MATHAMAGICAL II

ANAGRAMAPHOBIA
at word's end

by

Colin Davies

Cover Design by Colin Davies
Original Character Illustrations by Lindsey Boon
Illustration on chapter 'ST' by Heather Stephenson
Proof Readers - Barbara Wilkie and Moyra Davies
Edited by Ashley R Lister

Published by Wordrabbit Books Via Lulu.com
Print Edition: ISBN-13: 978-1-291-41314-4

Colin Davies
is a successful and highly respected author, poet and playwright. He was born in Brighton in 1970 and moved to Blackpool in 1988 where he lives with his partner and son. He writes in many different genres and styles however, he maintains that his heart can always be found in his children's stories and poetry.

Colin sits on the committee of the Lancashire Dead Good Poets' Society. He writes regular blog posts for the award-winning website deadgoodweb.co.uk and altblackpool.co.uk and he has been instrumental in helping local poets into positions as writers in residence.

Acknowledgements and Thanks

There are so many people to thank with regards to this book. Big thanks and hugs to my mother for doing such a great job of proofreading, and raising me of course. To Barbara Wilkie for her wonderful proofing of the first draft. I also want to thank my editor Ashley R Lister, not only is he a fantastic writer but also one of the best editors around, as well as being a very good friend. A big tip to any young writers out there: get to know at least two excellent proofreaders and one amazing editor.

I also need to thank my partner Heather Brennan for putting up with me when I'm in writing mode and for the valuable input and suggestions from the first read.

A very big thank you goes out to the talented Heather Stephenson who has produced a wonderful piece of artwork that can be found on chapter 'SP'. I will acknowledge that using pairs of letter to name chapters in a book is a little odd however, it works with the theme.

One person to whom I have to give a very big thank you is my good friend Tony McMullen. His flippant remark about 'what's really scary' was the seed I needed to bring this story to life and his comments and observations during the writing process where more than useful.

More thanks to Jennifer Ireland who gave me the original inspiration to start writing this series. To all my very good friends Mick Arthur, Dylan Freeman, Matthew Bartlett, Chris Giles and all the members of the Lancashire Dead Good Poets' Society. Your belief in my ability to tell this story has always been an inspiration.

Finally, but by no means least, I want to thank everyone who bought and read *Mathamagical*. The comments and feedback I have had made me want to continue this series, I truly hope you all enjoy reading this latest adventure for Ben Small and Adder.

Colin Davies, 2013

This book is dedicated to
Alan, Gary, Sean and Peter

Chapter AB

"Now, where do I start?"

Ben examined the trail of destruction left by his friends. Empty bottles of pop, half eaten bags of crisps and piles of biscuit crumbs randomly scattered on the carpet, CD's and computer games were not in their boxes like they should have been, instead they had made camp on the floor. Who'd have thought that five boys, who had just entered their teenage years, could have made so much mess in such a short period of time?

It had been his birthday party, so to speak, but instead of cake and ice cream he was allowed to have some friends for a sleep over to listen to music and play computer games without being troubled by adults. The one downside of this deal was that he had agreed to straighten out any untidiness his celebrations might have left.

Now surveying the task at hand he figured that this job was going to take longer than he had first anticipated and realised that his mother's predictions of the state of his room were in fact, correct.

Ben sat on his bed, in his left hand he held the roll of black bin liners that he had found in the cupboard under the kitchen sink and with a sharp tug, ripped off one of the bags. He placed the rest of the roll on his pillow and opened up the plastic sack that would be the last resting-place of the discarded munchies and the wrappers that first dressed them.

Dropping the bin liner to the floor he decided to start by picking up all the stuff that wasn't going to be thrown away. This involved finding the right box to correspond with the appropriate CD, DVD or game. After each disc was returned to its correct cover, the box was then relocated to a suitable place on the shelf from which it had originally come.

A number of books had also made their way from his well-ordered shelf to various locations in his quarters. Ben was somewhat confused by this as he didn't remember anybody reading any books. He gathered them together before spending several minutes making sure they went back in exactly the right place.

Just as he was slotting the last one back with the others he stopped, blinked, and shook his head. For a split second he was sure the title on the spin read 'GUMBO POSSE' instead of 'GOOSEBUMPS'.

Ben removed the book from the shelf again to examine the front cover. It was fine. 'GOOSEBUMPS' was written in green dripping slime just under R. L. Stine's black printed header. The picture of two green clawed hands opening a closet from the inside was surrounded by a pink slimy frame and the title, How to Kill a Monster, was there in white bold text at the bottom.

"I must be tired." He said to himself, once again placing the book back in his collection.

The discarded food wrappers and drinks bottles still decorated his carpet with a rubbish tip theme. Ben drew in a deep breath to ready himself for the second part of the task.

"Right!" he said picking up a bin liner, "Time to get busy."

Four hours, three bin liners, one duster and half a can of air freshener later the domain that Ben called his own was once again fit to sleep in. Nobody would ever have thought that one young boy resided here let alone, only twenty four hours earlier five such occupants had been living the high life for the night.

Ben was proud of his achievement and knew his mother would be delighted with his efforts, though he also knew she would expect him to keep it this way. He also knew that by the end of the week it would return to the state he normally left it in. This of course was a fraction of the mess he had just tidied up nevertheless, his mother would myther him about it until she wore him down and, reluctantly, he would concede, roll up his sleeves and once more tackle the residue of a normal boy's life.

The aroma of dinner had made its way up to the top floor, down the corridor and into Ben's room. This signalled the departure from his newly cleaned sleeping quarters and with a skip in his step, the journey to the kitchen had begun.

After a fine Sunday dinner with roast beef, roasted potatoes, carrots and Yorkshire pudding all covered with lovely thick beef gravy, followed by his Mums homemade apple pie smothered with thick yellow creamy custard, Ben retired to the sitting room to watch some TV.

At about 9 o'clock he wished his parents a good night then returned to his clean and tidy bedroom to prepare his bag for school the following day after which, he would read for about half an hour then sleep.

He studied the timetable blue-tacked to the wall over his desk. This gave Ben the information he required in selecting the right books and equipment for his day of learning.

He used his finger to ensure he was reading the right day and spoke to himself to make double sure he got the information correct.

"Right," he whispered, "Morning, double maths followed by history."

After his adventures with Adder, Ben rather enjoyed mathematics, his new understanding had been rewarded with a move to a higher class.

Ben stopped for a moment; he had just realised that it had been some time since he last saw his friend.

Adder had visited Ben on several occasions since their trip to Mathamagical. The two of them would sit in the field attached to the school and talk about what had been happening in each of the worlds. In fact, now Ben came to think of it, Adder the talking snake and General of the Mathamagical armies had visited him at least once every couple of weeks since they first met. Yet it must have been over two months since Ben had seen him. With his birthday bash to organise he hadn't notice the snake's absence.

"He must be busy that's all."

He opened the drawer of his bedside cabinet. Underneath his school tie was the infinity pin badge, he smiled.

"Yeah," he said comforting himself, "Just been busy."

Ben returned to his timetable. History took him up to morning break then English after the recess. He finished packing his bag and placed it by the door to his room, that way he knew he wouldn't forget it.

He'd had a bath earlier in the day so all that was left to do was brush his teeth, put his pyjamas on and get into bed. Before returning to Philip Pullman's Northern Lights, a book he was really enjoying, Ben set the time on him new alarm clock.

Being as he was a big fan of Doctor Who his parents had given him a talking Dalek clock for his birthday. The hands told the time over the face which had a picture of the Doctor's most notorious enemy staring straight out, while another Dalek rocked left and right on top in time with the seconds. To wake the sleeper up in the morning the makers had programmed in three phases that would play at random. All of which emanated from the time device in the hard scratchy electronic voice of these futuristic killers.

Ben had great fun pressing the test button and getting it to say, "You are the enemy of the Daleks, you must be destroyed!", "You would make a good Dalek!" or his favourite, "Exterminate!"

His friends had thought it was great too and at various points in the evening the conversation would be broken, as someone would press the button and make the Dalek interrupt. This was always greeted with the rest of the room repeating the phrase in a similar vocal style.

He set his wake-up time for seven o'clock in the morning, this would give him plenty of time to wash, get dressed, eat his breakfast and walk to school, as long as the weather was fine.

Getting himself comfortable, Ben opened up his book at the page he'd marked from Friday. The half an hour Ben had set aside became double that as he became engrossed with Lyra and her adventures.

Chapter CD

Adder stopped suddenly, the noise of the night creatures that occupied the forest had fallen unnaturally silent. Snap! He turned to look back at his party. Four Alpha guardsmen looked back him, the dim glow of their light orbs throwing shadows that hid their fear. The general used his tail to give a signal indicating that they should all crouch down. The letters obliged without argument.

He then gave the signal for them to wait and stay very still. This was an order they had no intention of breaking. Adder slid slowly forward through the woodland, his eyes twitched to see every slight movement in the foliage, his tongue flicked in and out of his mouth trying to detect any scents.

Suddenly he stopped, there was no sound but he was sure he felt something. He held his breath; there it was again, a low deep rumble, like something very big landing on the ground very hard.

The sound of cracking wood turned his attention to his right. Falling away to their left and right the trees of Paragraph Forest snapped under the intense pressure applied to them by the creature heading in Adder's direction.

The site was too much for the G guard at the rear of the party. Panic took over.

"RAID PESTGIN!" he shouted, before turning and running as fast as he could back from whence they had come.

The other Alphas started to back up in the same direction. Adder turned towards his deserting soldiers.

"STOP!" he commanded. "You are the enemy of the Daleks, you must be destroyed!"

Ben opened his eyes, his breathing was short and erratic, beads of sweat dampened his brow.

"Adder," he whispered.

"Exterminate!"

The Doctor Who alarm clock was on the second phrase of its wakeup procedure as programmed by Ben. He clasped his hands over his face and tried to rub away the feeling of dread the nightmare had left on him.

"You would make a good…" with his right hand he reached out and stopped the metallic voice saying anymore.

Ben hated nightmares; they always left him feeling detached from reality, as if he was still in a dream. He sat up in bed and scratched his head, yawned, then threw back the covers so he could begin the ritual of getting ready for school.

Having packed his school bag the night before all Ben had to do was get washed, get dressed and get breakfast, a routine he had perfected over the years.

He gathered up his school clothes and ventured out into the hallway. The sounds of breakfast television mumbled from downstairs indicating his mother was already up and about. The door to his parent's room was slightly ajar and from within he could hear the heavy breathing of Stephen's slumber.

His stepfather wasn't much of a morning person. Only on the very odd occasion Ben would see him at the kitchen table for breakfast. Most times it would be a quick, *"See ya tonight!"* as he ran out the door at 8 o'clock. Ben could never imagine getting up and ready five minutes before having to leave the house.

He carried on his short walk to the bathroom. Over the last year Ben had tried many different combination of shower, teeth, hair, clothes. First he had tested going for a shower, brushing his teeth and combing his hair then returning to his bedroom to put on his school clothes. After a number of months he changed it to getting dressed, going to the bathroom, getting undressed again, cleaning his teeth, standing under the shower, getting dressed then sorting his hair out. Finally he tried taking his clothes to the bathroom and getting ready after brushing his teeth in the shower then sorting his hair out after getting dressed, this was the best sequence of events he had found so far and, this morning, was the technique he used.

Once ready he returned to his room to collect his bag, the dream passed through his mind again. He walked over to his bedside cabinet and opened the draw. From under a small plastic bag full of rubber bands, a notebook that he used to write his things to do lists and an assortment of pens, Ben retrieved his gold infinity pin badge. Something was troubling him, maybe it was the dream or maybe it was not seeing Adder for so long. He shook his head and attached the infinity symbol to the left lapel of his blazer. With a deep breath he picked up his bag and made his way downstairs for breakfast.

Just as he was biting into a slice of toast covered with a thick layer of strawberry jam Stephen rushed past the open door of the kitchen. With his usual farewell he grabbed his coat and left. Shortly after the front door clicked shut the sound of Stephen's car revved up outside. Ben shook his head in disapproval of this rushing around. He finished his toast and tea then, kissing his mother on the check, set out for another day of learning.

The day was clear with a slight breeze coming from the north. This made the temperature chillier than the bright sunshine made it appear so Ben had to do up his blazer. His walk was as normal, nothing interesting was happening though Ben found himself glancing under every bush. He thought the sound of the breeze making its way calmly though the leaves of the trees sounded like a voice.

"Ben" it hushed.

He stopped for a moment to listen again, this time it was just a rustling. That dream has really affected me today he thought.

At the school gates Ben met his friends that had been round on Saturday night. They all laughed about the shenanigans that had taken place.

"And we completed Stuntman," Danny Kenman said with pride.

"Well we did," retorted Max Brandridge "You just sat there stuffing your face with crisps all night."

The group of friends laughed while Danny patted his full bodied figure and wrinkled up his nose making piggy noises.

"Too right I did!"

After registration Ben and his classmates went to Mrs Bowland's mathematics class. She was a stern woman, her grey hair tied back in a bun and wire framed glasses perched on the bridge of her small chiselled nose. They were either too big or her head had shrunk since she acquired them as during the lesson she spent most of the time pushing them back up with the index finger of her left hand.

Ben didn't mind double maths, Adder had taught him well and, even though he wasn't the quickest at arithmetic in the class, he would usually get all the answers right in his written work.

The hour went quite quickly and ended in the usual way. Scraping chairs and indefinable conversations filled the air while Mrs Bowland shouted over the top of the noise what she wanted the children to do for their homework in time for the next lesson. Ben packed his books into his bag, waited for the room to clear, then left.

Next it was history for half an hour before morning break. Mr Gregory, a softly spoken man who always wore blown jumpers that look a little bit tatty, started the lesson by announcing that next week there would be a field trip.

"As you know," he said using his hands to emphasise his phrasing, "We have been studying the man made tor that is know locally as Bell Hill"

With this he wrote Bell Hill on the blackboard in chalk, then as he spoke he wrote more words on the board to exact the same effect as he did with his hands.

"Now this is what is going to Happen. Next Monday we are going to Walk up the Tor to See the old stone Remains of the lookout Tower that used to stand there."

Ben looked at the blackboard the words Bell Hill, Happen, Monday, Walk, Tor, See, Remains and Tower were scrawled randomly across its surface. He looked down at the notebook on his desk. For some reason he'd written some of the words onto the red cover. Bell, Happen, See. This made no sense to him so he positioned his pen to scribble them out.

Just then the letters began to move. Ben glanced around the classroom, Mr Gregory was still waffling on about the trip and the other pupils were engrossed in what the teacher had to say. Ben returned to the moving letters.

They had begun to rearrange themselves. He blinked and shook his head. The B from Bell stayed in position at the beginning of the words with the E following it, the other letters glided like oil floating on the top of water until after a couple of seconds instead of Bell Happen See, it read, Ben   Please Help.

        "Adder!" Ben said, louder than he would have wanted to had he thought about it.

The class fell silent and everyone, including the teacher, glared at him. The uncomfortable feeling Ben always had when so many people paid him attention manifested. He knew something was wrong with his friend in the lands past the door in the skirting board. That feeling of dread after the nightmare made some sort of sense now. His only problem was, he couldn't do anything about it until after the lesson.

The thirty minutes felt like hours, nothing Mr Gregory said registered with Ben. All he could think about was getting to the science room and getting back to Mathamagical.

The bell rang indicating a halt to proceedings and the beginning of a fifteen-minute respite from the gaining of knowledge. However, whereas the other pupils had thoughts of running around in the fresh air, eating crisps or standing around talking about the latest bands in the charts, Ben headed straight for the science room.

He'd managed to slip his friends in the shuffle that ensued when everybody left the classroom by taking a quick left out of the door and then running as fast as he could to the corner of the next corridor. Here he turned a sharp right, nearly falling over as he did. This was the linking throughway between two of the buildings. Down each side for the entire distance the upper half of the walls were made up of large windows fitted side by side so close as to have no gaps.

Ben focused on the other end and ran. He had no time to waste; he had to be in the science room, reduced in size and through the door before break was over. At the end of the glass corridor Ben took a sharp left then right, this took him up a set stairs, which turned back on themselves halfway up to the next floor. At the top he turned right and, without stopping pushed open the double doors.

Only the doors didn't fly open as Ben had expected, instead they moved slightly then shut again accompanied by a thud followed by the sound of someone falling over and dropping a large amount of paper.

Ben sheepishly pushed the door and peered through the gap. Sitting on the smooth shiny floor of the corridor was Mr Trot surrounded by the papers and leaver files he had been carrying. The science teacher looked up at Ben with a very angry expression.

"Was that you?"

Ben entered the corridor, "Sorry sir." He said hanging his head in embarrassment. He knew what it was like to be knocked over by someone else opening a door, "Are you Okay?"

"I think so," Mr Trot sounded a bit calmer now. "Where are you going in such a hurry?"

Ben had to think quickly, he could hardly say that his friend, a talking snake, was in trouble in a world he could only get to by going through a door hidden in the skirting board at the back of the science room. He needed a better excuse.

"Mr Granville," he started, his voice a bit shaky as lying was a skill he had never been very good at, "asked me to get him, umm, something from the, umm, science room."

Mr Trot started to pick up his papers; Ben bent down to help.

"Don't mind that," Mr Trot waved Ben away with his hand, "you can't keep the headmaster waiting. Go on, the door's open."

"Thank you sir and, I am really sorry."

Mr Trot smiled at Ben in a polite way then turned his attention back to retrieving his documents. Ben turned and stared towards the science room only, instead of running he just walked, all be it at a brisk pace.

By the time he'd got as far as the broken chair that marked the whereabouts of the science room door, Mr Trot had gathered his stuff together and continued his journey through the school.

Ben entered the classroom, he had been in here many, many times since that fateful night and every time he was in here he glanced down at the small door. It was so obvious to him yet no one else saw it, and he never pointed it out.

At the back of the class Ben readied himself. He had his bag, his pens and his wits; I don't need anything else he thought. He rubbed the infinity badge on his lapel with his thumb, drew in a deep breath and recited the ratio spell.

"Ten to one, one to ten, Scale down Ben Small to this ratio."

With the last word uttered everything around Ben started to grow bigger. He had forgotten about the weird feeling in his stomach and didn't really like it too much. Seconds later he was ten times smaller. He walked up to the door in the skirting board and opened it. Through the opening he could see the zero path with the black positive lands to the right and the red negative landscape to the left.

He stepped forward to enter the world of Mathamagical once more, as he advanced through the doorway he banged his head on the top of the frame.

"Ouch!" He said rubbing the bump, "That never happened last time?"

Then he realised, it had been almost a two years since he was last here and in that time he'd grown a bit taller. The ratio spell would have to be recalculated to make him the size he was before.

"There's no time for that now," he said dipping his head so he didn't bang it again, "Adder needs me."

Ben stepped forward onto the Zero path. The door disappeared behind him, from the sign by the side of the pathway he could see the direction he needed to go and without delay, set about his journey back to the city of numbers.

Chapter EF

The sun was high in the sky and the air was warm. A flock of black positive birds observed the young boy hurrying down the road from their vantage point high in a multiply sign tree, on the other side of the path an identical flock of red negative birds followed suit. Ben was oblivious to this; all he was concerned about was getting to the city and finding Adder.

He tried running for a bit but the heat of the day, and his memory of how far he had to go slowed him down to a brisk walk. I wish I'd brought some water, he thought as the temperature and exercise combined to make him thirsty.

Putting these feeling to one side he strode forward making good time. Even though his pace was far quicker than the first time he made this journey, to Ben, it felt much longer. Seeing the gates at the end of the green path filled him with relief for having reached the city at last and, a warm sense of nostalgia. His memories of the city were some of the best times he had ever had and, even though the circumstances of his visit worried him, he was glad to be back.

Somewhat tired from his journey Ben approached the gates. The enormity of the entrance was as impressive as the first time. With his right hand clenched in a first he banged on the gates.

The sound of large metal bolts being drawn back echoed from the other side. The gate slowly creaked open. Through the gap hopped forward an Ohm guard.

"Halt!" he commanded, "Who wishes entry to Mathamagical?"

"I am Ben Small," The boy said with a respectful yet authoritarian tone, "Friend of General Adder, Pi and the Prime Numbers."

With his right hand he pulled the left lapel of his blazer forward to show the Ohm his infinity badge.

The guard looked the boy up and down four times before approaching him. Ben was beginning to get frustrated by the delay but knew he had to go through the routine. They couldn't just let him in without being sure.

The guard took a long hard look at the badge decorating Ben's school uniform. The boy smiled then polished the gold with him right sleeve.

The Ohm looked up at Ben, "Where are you going?" he asked.

"3.141593 Tangent Avenue," Ben replied, "The home of Pi. I need to speak to him and the members of the Round Circle."

The Ohm guard looked Ben up and down once more then, with all the respect a private gives an officer, stepped back and to one side.

"You may enter, Mr Small, sir!"

Ben nodded in appreciation, "Thank you."

He took a moment to gather his thoughts, just long enough to count to ten but not so long that the Ohm would start wondering about the delay.

The old stone, fortified guardhouse was a hive of activity. Ohms were going about their business with a regimented precision that only an army could organise. The deep low boom of the gate being closed hung in the air like a rumble of thunder in the distance. It reminded Ben of the creature looming over Adder in his dream.

He wasted no time and headed straight for the door that led out to the main circular of the city. Coming out from the dullness of the gatehouse, the bright colours of the buildings, extenuated by strength of the sunlight, caused Ben to squint.

The busy populace of Mathamagical filled the street, all looking like they had somewhere to be. The road was full of vehicles travelling in each direction. By the height of the sun, and the amount of people on the street, Ben figured it must be lunchtime.

After taking a few seconds to get his bearing Ben turned left and headed towards Tangent Avenue.

The heat was getting to get to Ben, he removed his blazer and hooked it over his left arm. This time he was prepared for the strange looks he knew were coming his way. Although he still didn't like the attention, there were far more important matters at hand and he would not let the curiosity of others bother him.

The people on the streets were different from the last time he visited the city. Since the alliance of the Alphas, Algebras and Numerics the city streets were no longer just filled with Numbers and Maths Symbols. Now there were letters walking amongst them living their day to day lives. Ben noticed that the all letters he saw were the pastel coloured Algebra citizens. Not once on his journey around the long outer circular road nor, after turning right at the bright red five story building that marked the corner of Tangent Avenue, did he see one single brightly coloured Alpha.

Even though he found this odd his mind was too preoccupied to consider what it meant. He continued down the Avenue in the direction of the city centre until he found what he was searching for. At the top of the concrete steps Pi's green door, decorated with the brass number 3.141593, advertised the entrance to the purple painted headquarters of the Round Circle.

He climbed the steps and pressed the brass button fixed to the wall on the right of the door. From deep within, the distant tinkling sound of the bell rang to alert the occupants that someone wished to be seen.

The wait, which Ben was expecting, made him anxious. It had just dawned on him how much trouble he was going to be in back home. Not only was he going to be home very late, he was now missing from school.

        "I'm going to be suspended for sure," he whispered to himself, "and this time for a good reason."

He rang the bell again, this time the tinkling sound was followed by the unmistakable voice of Pi. "Alright, alright, I'm coming."

The locks clicked and the door opened inwards, there in the hallway was

Ben's constant friend. Pi took a moment to look the boy up and down then down and up.

"BEN!" he exclaimed, his voice full of joyful surprise, "What are you doing here? It's so great to see you, come in, come in."

Ben went into the house without hesitation. "It's good to see you again Pi."

The old symbol closed the front door then took the lead through to the room at the back of the house where the Round Table Committee met. Sir Cumferance was the first to notice Ben, which he did with much excitement. His clapping hands alerted Dye Ameter and Ray Dius to the boy's presence.

Before Ben could say anything he was surrounded by the committee members all patting him on the back, shaking his hand and asking how are you? and what do we owe the pleasure of this visit?

Pi could see how overwhelmed Ben was by this greeting and, sounding like a teacher trying to restore order in a classroom full of over excited children, asked the group for some decorum, "Will you lot let the boy sit down?"

Pi's command was greeted with silence and expressions only usually seen on the faces of children who have just been stopped from doing something they found to be fun. This was followed by obedience and the members of the round circle backed away from Ben allowing him into the room. Dye pulled out a chair and beckoned Ben to sit.

Ben smiled, "Thank you Dye," he said accepting the invitation, "And it's really good to see all of you again."

Everybody returned to their normal positions around the large round table. Ben scanned from left to right; his feelings of joy for seeing them all again were mixed with worry for Adder. Pi could see this mixed emotion on the boy's face.

"What's troubling you Ben?"

"Adder," replied Ben, "Where is he?"

Dye stood up and started to walk around the table in a clockwise direction.

His Welsh accent took on an official tone, "General Adder has gone to Alphabet City. He left last week with the rest of the Alphas."

"And why has he gone there?" asked Ben.

"Apparently they've been having a bit of trouble in their outer townships," Dye completed one full circuit of the table, "And they came asking for help."

Ray continued the story from his seated position, "You know what Adder's like. He immediately volunteered his services."

"We all offered to go along," explained Dye now starting his second rotation, "But Adder was having none of it."

Sir Cumference looked straight at Ben, "He said it was something or nothing. All the Alphas needed was some organisation."

"You know the General," said Pi, "always willing to help."

"So he's not here you see." Dye had just started his third trip round when he looked at Pi; the symbol pointed at him, then at the seat Dye had previously occupied. "I know, I know, time to sit down."

Dye returned to his place at the table. Ben looked down to gather his thoughts; there had been Alpha guards in his dream and a big creature. Now Ben was beginning to realise that it wasn't his imagination that had created that scene.

"Adder's in trouble." He said without raising his head.

"What?" gasped the members of the committee in unison.

"I think," Ben looked up at the shocked expression being worn by the others, "I know he's been captured by something."

He began to tell the Round Circle Committee about the dream and the message sent via the jumbled up words. For some reason his mind was drawn back to the Goosebumps book the day before, how the title had been scrambled.

"This trouble the Alpha's are having," started Ben, "Does it involve letters being mixed up?"

"Yes," said Pi, "Their outer townships are where the words live. The Alphas said that these words had become messed up, letters in the wrong order making different words."

Ben's mind was racing, "And that's why Adder thought they just needed some organisation?"

"His words precisely," said Sir Cumferance.

"I have to go to Alphabet City," Ben's voice had taken on a very serious tone, "I have to go there now."

He stood up from the table and placed his hands, palms down, on its surface. He was never one for being overly brave but this was Adder, his friend, and no matter what dangers lay in wait he was not going to let him down.

"I need you to tell me how to get there?"

Pi stood up, "I'll do better than that Ben, I'm coming with you."

"No," said Ben, "I can't ask you to…"

Pi interrupted, "You're not asking, I'm telling you."

Ben smiled; the prospect of going alone had filled him with dread. Now with Pi as a companion he felt more confident.

"The rest of you," Pi addressed the other members, "Will stay here and wait for our message. If we all go there will be no one to advise the Prime Numbers and depending on what we find out, we may need their help."

Sir Cumferance, Dye Ameter and Ray Dius reluctantly agreed. They were all friends of Adder and all wanted to do what they could to help. Ben rummaged through his bag and pulled out a pen and notepad. Flicking through the pages he found one that had not yet been used.

Along the top line he wrote *'Things we need'*. After he had underlined this with two straight blue lines, he started on his list which would be pretty similar to the ones he wrote out for camping.

Pi's house was like a bric-a-brac shop, every room was full of stuff that most people would have thrown away long ago. There were shelves full of old books, ornaments made from various metals and porcelain, boxes full of picture postcards and old tools, Ben didn't know where to start.

"Leave it to us," said Pi, "Just tell us what's on your list."

Ben started to read, "A compass; a telescope; some rope; water bottle; a penknife; a map; a small mirror and a towel."

As Ben read out each item one of the Round Circle members would disappear into a room. Banging and crashing noises of things being picked up and moved would bellow forth before the member returned with the requested item. Everything on the list was gathered, all except the map.

"Why do you need all this stuff?" enquired Ray.

"The compass is to find out which direction we are heading;" Ben explained picking up the compass and demonstrating, this he did with every item. "The telescope is to see into the distance; the pen knife should we need to cut something; the small mirror for sending signals and seeing around corners and the water bottle in case we get thirsty."

"Why do we need a towel?" asked Pi.

"You always need a towel," replied Ben. "What if we get wet? Now, what about the map?"

"We don't need a map," replied Pi, "I know where Alphabet City is."

Ben sighed "It's not for finding the City, it's for the area around it."

"Oh," said Pi, "I don't have one of those."

"Never mind we might get one from the Alphas."

"Or a guide," said Dye, "They might send someone with you to show you around."

Ben removed his schoolbooks from his bag and replaced them with the items for the journey.

Pi went to the kitchen to fill the water bottle, whilst there he made some cheese sandwiches for when they got hungry. He knew it would take them more than a day to get over the hill and didn't like the idea of missing his tea.

He returned to the room where Ben was making his final checks and handed him the water and food.

Ben smiled, he'd forgotten about eating and was glad Pi had remembered.

He threw the bag over his shoulder; it was slightly lighter than when it was full of his school books. They left 3.141593 Tangent Avenue and headed back along the streets towards the main gates. Ray, Dye and Sir Cumferance came along to wish them well on their travels.

At the guardhouse Pi spoke with the captain of the Ohms. Moments later the gate was opened. Ben thought back to the time when he and Adder joined the Crystal 1 here. They were going to talk to the Alphas then as well, only this time they had further to walk.

The two said their farewells and stepped forward back onto the Zero path.

"So where do we go from here?" Ben asked Pi.

"Straight along the Zero path until the road turns red and the lands either side of it are green."

On the right a small black positive fox scurried away from the path and hid under a black Plus sign bush. On the left an identical Negative fox did the same.

"Best foot forward." Said Pi, walking on as the booming sound of the gate closing behind them filled the air.

Ben whispered under his breath, "We're coming Adder."

Chapter GH

Ben checked the little bass compass retrieved from Pi's hoard. According to the little arrow they were heading north. He looked round to check the position of the setting sun. Unlike the sun back home it was starting its descent to the east and, judging from its height above the horizon, it wouldn't be long before nightfall.

The heavy heat was beginning to recede with the day's end and even though the sky was clear, the temperature was very pleasant. As the daylight turned to the reddish hues of dusk, Ben and Pi made the decision to rest and stopped by the side of the road. They had travelled way past the signpost that marked Ben's entrance to this world and were now high up the hillside. The City of Numbers was a distant memory of the landscape, only countryside occupied the vista in every direction.

Dusk turned to night and the large bright full moon, rising in the west, removed the colours around them turning everything into various shades of grey. A red negative owl hooted from a distant treetop far off to the left, at the same time a similar sound came from the black lands on the right.

The moon was bright enough for the two to see so Ben didn't bother getting out his torch. *No need to waste the batteries*, he thought. The heat of the day and the travelling had made both of them tied. Ben turned to ask Pi a question only to be greeted by a loud grunt followed by a deep snore from his companion. Poor Pi was so tired that he had drifted off to the land of nod without a word of goodnight.

Ben positioned his bag under his head like a pillow and lay back. The night's sky was awash with stars, he wondered if, like back in his world, they had names for all of them.

Sitting up straight Ben awoke with a start, he hadn't even realised he'd fallen asleep. The morning sun was bright and it took a moment for him to take stock of where he was. Pi was already awake and tucking into a cheese sandwich.

"Breakfast," he said offering one of the sandwiches to Ben.

Ben took the food. "Thank you," he said with a slight croak to his voice.

"We should be there by nightfall," Pi assured Ben, "if we keep up the pace from yesterday."

Ben finished his sandwich, took a small drink of water then returned everything to his bag.

Pi didn't push Ben to get going; he'd been awake for the sunrise about an hour earlier. He figured that Ben needed his sleep and so didn't disturb him. The way the young lad had woken up Pi also reckoned Ben needed a few minutes to get his bearing before they continued.

They set off north again, the green brick path leading them up the largest of the hills. Pi asked Ben about his homeland. Ben was more than please to talk about it. He told Pi about his place of learning, about the teachers and how they taught them stuff like history, geography and science. This fascinated pi; all they learnt at Mathamagical School were the rules of mathematics and how to be a good citizen.

Being as history was one of Ben's best subjects he decided to spend the time telling Pi about his favourite periods of time, the Middle Ages, and proceeded to spin yarns of kings and queens, knights on horseback and legends of valour.

Ben was so enthusiastic about telling his stories and Pi was so enraptured by the tales, neither of them noticed how long they'd been walking. By the time they were aware of their surroundings they had reached the summit of the hill. Stretching out before them over the brow the land of the Alphas spread out in all directions.

The positive and negative lands had become lush green meadows with a red brick path winding its way down through the hills and across the plains. In the distance the City of Letters reached up to the sky. Tall sharp buildings surrounded by a dark grey stone wall. From the vantage point occupied by the two travellers the entire cityscape could be seen. Ben looked down at the path, it changed from green to red with a very definitive line at the very top of the hill. He looked left then right, the line continued across the tops of all of the hills, themselves lining up creating a natural border. The divide, as straight as any ruler, with the colour changing from either the black of the negative side or red of the positive to green. The sharpness of the divide reminded Ben of the lines draw on a map to indicate county or country borders.

The two stepped forward over the line, instantly the temperature of the air changed. The warmth that had accompanied the sunshine disappeared and left behind a cold chill. Ben knew something was amiss, this cold was not natural. He removed the telescope from his bag. Holding the small end to his left eye he surveyed the city. Even with the magnifier Ben couldn't make out the finer details.

He returned the telescope to his bag and turned to Pi. The symbol's expression was one of discomfort; he obviously didn't like the unnatural feeling of the cold.

"Something bad is happening here," said Pi, "I've been here before and it wasn't cold like this."

"Come on," said Ben stepping forward, "There's only one way to find out for sure."

He repositioned his bag on his shoulder to make it more comfortable and headed off down the hill. Pi took a deep breath and, mustering up all of his courage, followed.

The biting breeze made the journey very unpleasant. Ben tried to tell more stories about the really old days but the ambiance that befell these lands made it rather difficult find the words. After a short while he decided to give up talking and just put his head down and walked.

Time seemed to pass slowly, Ben checked the compass, they were now heading east. The meadows, though beautiful in colour with little yellow and blue flowers, seemed somehow harsh, void of wildlife. There were no birds flying by, no rabbits burrowing; it was like they had all left. It reminded Ben of Narnia only without the snow, a kind of permanent winter.

They didn't stop for lunch or tea, instead they ate on the move. The sun moved across the sky but failed to penetrate the cold with its warmth.

The colours of dusk radiated from the sun's hiding place behind Alphabet City as the two travellers reached the gate at the end of the red path. Two enormous wooden doors at least one hundred metres tall filled a dark grey stone archway, a large capital 'A' motif straddled the join in the middle. It reminded Ben of the old castle gates he'd seen on many drawing of the past.

Attached to the wall to the right of the gate, a bell hung with a rope attached to its clapper. Ben walked over and shook the rope, which in turn hit the clapper off the side of the bell causing it to ring.

The harsh metallic sound broke the silence of the countryside in a most dramatic way, which, once Ben had finished ringing it, exaggerated the silence once more.

The breeze whistled by. After what seemed like minutes rather than seconds, a small door, about the size of Ben's head, opened in the gate.

"Who goes there!?" a stern voice within demanded.

Ben stepped forward, "I am Ben, Ben Small and this is Pi. We have come from Mathamagical in search of General Adder. He came this way last week to help you with your troubles."

The small door slammed shut with a loud bang. Ben looked over at Pi; he just shrugged his shoulders. A loud metallic clunk came from behind the wooden barriers. In silence Ben and Pi watched as the right hand gate slowly creaked open. Through the gap advanced a pale blue upper-case T wearing a grey tin helmet decorated with a light grey feather sticking out of the top.

"Ben Small," the letter began with a deep knowledgeable voice, "I am commander T of the Eighth Chapter Division. We've been expecting you."

"Me!" Ben said, pointing at himself.

"General Adder said you'd come if things went wrong," he paused for a moment, "and from what we have heard today, things have gone very wrong indeed."

"Very wrong!" said Pi in a panic, "Where's Adder? What's *very wrong* mean? What's going on?"

"Calm down," Ben placed his hand on Pi's shoulder, "I'm sure the commander will tell us everything we need to know."

Ben glanced over at T and nodded as if to say: *that's right, isn't it?* The commander confirmed this to be true.

"Please," he said gesturing to the opening, "If you would just follow me this way."

Ben reassured Pi that everything was going to be all right then, leading the way, entered the city through the opening in the gates.

*****

Just like Mathamagical the entrance led to a fortified guardhouse only here the design was much more ornate. Large wonderfully carved statues of various letters overlooked the main room from their positions in the smooth dark grey walls.

Different letters wearing similar helmets, only with feathers in different shades of grey, went about their business in the same regimented fashion as the Ohms. The lighter grey feathers seemed to be in charge, barking out orders that the darker grey feathers obeyed without question. Ben noticed that all the letters were a pale colour, *More like the Algebras than the bright colours of the Alphas,* he thought.

Commander T ordered the gate to be closed. Four guardsmen ran over and grabbed the handle mounted to the inside. With an almighty heave they pulled the gate shut. A fifth guard standing over by the left-hand side pulled a lever and with a loud crunch and scrape, the large metal bolts that held the gate shut, were back in place.

"The council of vowels will want to see you."

The commanding T moved past the visitors and started to lead them across the room. Ben could see a normal sized door on the other side, *If this is the same as the Mathamagical guardhouse*, he thought, *then that leads out to the city*.

"I will summon you some transport," T said, before shouting out to some of the guards, "Get me a carriage and a driver round the front now!"

Ben felt a little embarrassed by the way T spoke to his men. *Okay this is the army*, he thought, *but it doesn't take much to say please*. They followed the commander over to the door. He placed his hand on the handle.

"Just wait by the front, your carriage will be here shortly," he said calmly, "and good luck."

With that he opened the door. The cold air swept in chilling the two guests to the bone. Ben looked at Pi, then at the commander. He felt a sense of déjà vu, once again he was entering a new city, a new land, and once again he was trying to save them. Only this time he had no idea what he was getting into, no rhyme to solve. He took a deep breath, counted to ten and stepped forward through the door.

Chapter IJ

They emerged from the entrance of the guardhouse to be greeted by a cold, desolate street. It was like a ghost town, nobody around; the only sound was the ice-cold breeze whistling through the enormous grey buildings which towered over the wall. Directly opposite them stood a huge ornate structure, dark grey in colour, with two spires that reached up higher than the other buildings on the street. A set of wide concrete steps led up to a wonderfully curved inset archway that was filled with two dark wooden doors; it reminded Ben of a church.

Everything was void of colour, the buildings, the road and the pavement; it made the wind feel even colder. This place wasn't a happy one and that feeling soon fell upon Pi and Ben.

A West Country voice echoed from side of the guardhouse breaking the silence.

"Walk on there!"

This was followed by what can only be described as the sound of hooves on cobbles. From behind the corner two large pale brown uppercase N's Trotted forward, behind them they pulled a four-wheeled wooden carriage. Perched in the driver's seat a pastel coloured lowercase d held the reins, mounted in a purpose built holder by his side, his whip. Using the reins he guided the N horses to the front of the guardhouse and brought them to a stop by the side of road where Ben and Pi stood.

"Woah there!"

Ben looked up at the driver; the drive in turn stared straight back at Ben then tipped his cap as way of a greeting. The N horses were restless, shuffling their feet and making snorting noises.

"They don't like being out too long," said the driver. "Not since all this began."

"My name is Ben," said the boy placing his right hand on his chest,

"And this is Pi."

"I know who you are," the lowercase d turned his attentions to the road ahead, "my job is to take you to the Council of Vowels. Now get on up here."

He pulled a lever that opened the carriage door.

Pi was just glad to be going somewhere that might get him out of the cold.

Before Ben could ask any questions his maths symbol friend was up and in the transport. In for a penny in for a pound, he thought then followed Pi.

"Walk on there!" came the command and, with a jerk as the N horses pulled forward, they were moving.

All the streets were the same dull grey in colour with not a soul to be seen. The N horses, under the guidance of the driver's reins, turned left, then right, then left again, deep into the heart of the city. Ben tried to ask the driver questions about what had happened but all he got in return was, 'You'll see,' and, 'Not my place to say.'

After about twenty minutes the carriage pulled up outside an official looking building with large uppercase A statute either side of the double doors, marking the entrance. The driver pulled his lever again allowing Ben and Pi to exit.

"Just through those doors there," he said without looking at his passengers, "Tell the receptionist who you are and ask to see the Council of Vowels."

Ben climbed down first, followed by Pi. The symbol wasn't as proficient getting out of the carriage as he was getting in and as the driver shouted, "Walk on there!" he lost his balance. The motion of the advance of the N horses caused him to spin which in turn flung the poor Round Circle dignitary into the back of Ben.

With a bump the two of them fell to the floor.

"Oh, I'm so sorry," apologised Pi, "I didn't mean to…"

"It alright Pi," Ben said sitting up, "it could happen to anyone."

They helped each other up and brushed themselves down before, with the sounds of the N horse hooves fading away in the distance, they climbed the steps and entered the building.

It was much warmer inside although everything was still grey. The walls, the chairs, even the receptionist's desk was grey. The only colour to be seen was that of the various letters walking this way and that, carrying pieces of paper from one room to another and they all looked rather pale. Ben told Pi to wait where he was and approached the faded yellow uppercase R sat behind the desk.

"Hello," he said in a soft voice, "I'm Ben Small and this is Pi, we're here to see the Council of Vowels."

The yellow R turned her attention away from the typewriter and looked up. Her reaction was the first suggestion of surprise Ben had encountered in the city. As with most of the inhabitants here, she would never have seen a human before yet, nobody else seemed to be bothered. Ben ran his finger round the inside of his collar. He really didn't like feeling out of place but needs must; he gathered his composure and repeated his opening statement.

"Mr Small," the R spoke with a sweet gentle tone, "I'll just check for you sir."

She stood up from behind her desk and walked down the corridor leading back into the building. Ben watched as she knocked on the door two down on the right. She paused as if waiting for something and then entered.

Ben walked over to Pi who was stood by the entrance reading a sign.

'All visitors to Alphabet House must sign in at reception. This is to ensure that everyone in the building can be accounted for should such terrible events arise such as

earthquake, fire or something darn right nasty. Thank you for your continued help in this matter, A (Leader of the council)'

"What do you think darn right nasty is?" Pi asked Ben.

"I don't know," replied Ben, "The driver that brought us here?"

Pi laughed out loud which made Ben giggle. For a moment the worries that the two had been carrying with them faded. A booming voice that emanated from the corridor snapped them back to reality.

"BEN SMALL!"

Ben turned round to see a stocky pale blue upper-case I marching down the hallway towards them. As he approached he thrust forward a hand in both greeting and friendship. Ben offered his right hand for the greeting, which the I took with great delight. The letter's grip was very firm, as was his shaking up and down with every word he spoke.

"Great to finally meet you," Ben's shoulder was beginning to hurt and he thought if this didn't end soon the I might pull his arm right out of its socket, "Adder has told me so much about you. And you must be Pi?"

Finally he let go and turned his attention to Pi who declined the handshake and opted for a simple wave. This seemed a much better idea to Ben and, rubbing his shoulder, wished he'd thought of it.

"Come," boomed the I, "you must meet the rest of the council."

With this the blue letter turned on his heels and marched back up the corridor. Ben looked over at Pi who in turned shrugged his shoulders. Knowing he had no other options, Ben straightened his blazer, made his bag comfortable and headed off in pursuit of the Vowel followed closely by Pi.

The pale blue I walked very quickly with huge purposeful strides. Ben and Pi struggled to keep up and had to resort to small bouts of running just to keep pace.

abcdefgh**ij**klmnopqrstuvwxyz

Down to the end of the main corridor, left, through a set of double doors, right. There was no time to take in any of the surroundings, the only things Ben noticed was the lack of colour. More lefts followed by more rights, it was hard to tell whereabouts in the building they were now.

Without warning the I stopped outside a door on the right, it was a good job Ben was paying attention otherwise he would have walked straight into him, unlike Pi who did exactly that. The stocky Vowel didn't even flinch as Pi rebounded from his body and ended up sitting on the floor.

"Are you alright there?" the letter enquired.

Pi picked himself back up again, with Ben's assistance, nodded to I then brushed himself down.

"You have to watch these floors," said the I pushing open the door, "Darn slippery things sometimes."

He entered the room, holding the door open waiting for the two to join him. Ben gestured for Pi to go first; everyone they'd met so far had been quite abrupt so Ben thought he'd inject a little politeness into proceedings.

Ben followed Pi into the room; it was large with many empty seats. At one end, off to the left, a long wooden table occupied a slightly raised area. Behind this four upper-case letters were seated. A pale green A and a pastel pink E were on the left with a light orange O and a faded purple U on the right. Ben figured that the empty chair in the middle would be were the   blue I sat.

"These must be the Council of Vowels," Ben whispered to Pi.

"What makes you think that?"

The I closed the door then made his way to the stage before taking his seat and proving Ben's theory correct.

"A, E, I, O and U. they are the only vowels in the alphabet."

"Oh," replied Pi learning something he didn't know.

The two walked up the room towards the stage. The E held up her hand in the way a police woman does to tell cars to stop.

"Wait!" she said in a firm voice, "You haven't been asked to approach the council yet."

This annoyed Ben; it was one thing having etiquette, he thought, but you need to be told the rules before you can obey them. Frustration was beginning to take over, nobody had said please or thank you since they got here, it was time to say something.

"Now look here," began Ben, "we have not travelled this far to be treated like this."

The shocked look on the faces of the council made Ben wish he'd been a bit more tactful. He looked across at Pi; an expression of surprise looked back at him. The faded purple U rose up from his chair.

"Please forgive us," He said softly, "These times in which we live have made us forget our manners."

I then spoke, "This is Ben Small, the one Z told us helped sort out that awful misunderstanding with the Numerics."

"The one Adder said would come should things be worse than he thought?" asked the A.

"Yes" replied the I.

The orange O looked worried, "So things are worse then?"

"Just because things are worse," E said in a stern way, "doesn't mean we shouldn't follow the rules of council."

"We must maintain order," said A.

Ben couldn't believe his ears, something was obviously very wrong here and his friend, following an attempt to help them out, was now in danger: and all they wanted to do was discuss how much worse things had got while following the rules of council.

"Poppycock!" he said in frustration before pointing this out.

"And how do you think he got into trouble?" E rhetorically asked, "By not following the rules. He just took off into the forest without submitting the correct forms filled in properly and passed by committee then…"

"Well maybe," Ben interrupted, "he thought that you didn't have enough time to do all that."

Ben approached the table and placed his hands, palms down, on the smooth surface.

"If someone could just explain what Adder was trying to help you with," he made a point of looking each member of the council in the eye as he spoke, "then we might be able to do something about it."

"You would need special clearance for that," said E, "we'd need forms B1, B2 and C6 filled in, then have them passed through the information committee who meet next Tuesday…"

"He already has clearance!"

Ben recognised the voice coming from the back of the room, Capital Z. He turned to see the leader of the Alphas but the site that greeted him left him aghast. Instead of the deep ruby colour he remembered the proud letter being he was now washed out, faded. Just then Ben realised that all the letters were paler than he remembered. Not only was the city void of colour but so were its inhabitants. Something was draining them, something that Adder was trying to sort out.

"What's happened here?" he asked Z.

"Follow me Ben," he said calling the boy over with his hand, "I'll explain everything."

Ben stepped down off the stage and gestured to Pi to follow as he passed.

"This is unprecedented!" complained E.

This comment sparked another row between the council members that continued even after Z, Ben and Pi had left the room. Not even the closed door could completely drown out their bickering.

The three walked along the corridor at a much better pace.

"They've been like that since it all started," Z explained, "only it's been getting worse. They can't get anything done, bogged down by protocol and procedure." He stopped and turned towards Ben, "The whole foundation of language is under threat."

Ben gulped; the leading letter's tone had such a futility about it he was beginning to wonder whether or not he could do anything. This wasn't just some puzzle to solve; it was obviously much darker than that.

They continued their journey to Z's office without saying another word. *Hang in there Adder*, he thought to himself, *I'll find some way of getting you out of this, mark my words.*

Z's office was like the rest of Alphabet City, grey and lifeless. Ben and Pi sat in chairs on one side of a large desk not dissimilar to the one in the headmaster's office at Cottomwall Grammar. Z took his position round the other side.

"It all started about three months ago," he said opening a draw in the desk, "Some of the Word villages reported that many of their citizens had become mixed up, made into words that made no sense."

Z placed a big black leather bound book on the desk. Embossed on the front in light grey were the letters A and Z.

"This continued, village after village reporting the same thing. We asked Mathamagical for help and Adder offered his services." Z opened the book, "Shortly after he left to investigate the colour started to drain from our world, that's when corporal G returned, he had gone with Adder and a small patrol from his platoon. What he told us sent people into a panic; they just stayed indoors. The only work being done round here are the brave guards looking after the defences and the people in this building." He gave out a big sigh. "Only the council have become obsessed with rules and regulation, they think that more order is needed to defeat this."

"And you don't agree?" asked Ben.

"Here," said Z turning then pushing the book across the top of the desk, "Read this."

Ben looked at the top of the page; a shiver ran down his spine. Ben knew the words that ran across the top of the page in bold black letters; he knew them because they had been in his dream.

"What's a Raid Pestgin?" asked Pi reading the book.

"The thing that killed Adder," replied Z.

"No!" Ben slammed his hand down on the book, "Adder is still alive!"

Z stared across the desk at Ben, "How can you be so sure?"

"He sent me a message."

For Ben to be of any help at all he had to know what he was up against. Making himself more comfortable, he shuffled in his seat and began to read about The legend of the Raid Pestgin.

Chapter KL

The Legend of the Raid Pestgin

Let no mistake be made, nor assumption be presumed, shall she return forth from the mountains with vengeance on her mind. Watch carefully for the signs be missed all good intention will decline, and chaos reign for she shall not rest until every word is rearranged and reading them becomes so hard, that words no more will inhabit these parts.

Her hidden name she keeps from thee so no magic can be thrown. Her return will bring about the fall of every language one and all, and this will come when upon the land her pet she sends to flatten all that stands in opposition.

For larger than a wolf or bear, bigger than the tallest tree, through the forest it shall walk, destruction in its wake, the last days signalled by its call.

Eight times its legs as thick as trees, its body fat and round, and jaws that could bite through the very walls round these city grounds. To defeat it you must know its name as the only way to send her back from whence she came and save all language for all time.

Raid Pestgin, Raid Pestgin, Raid Pestgin.

***

Ben sat back in his chair; beads of sweat damped his forehead. He turned to Pi, his symbol friend wore such a look of fear that Ben felt himself becoming scared.

Z broke the silence, "The beast is walking in the forest."

"I know," said Ben, "I saw it in my dream."

Ben's mind raced to think of any idea that could help. She, he thought, Who is she? He asked Z this same question.

Z began to tell the tale of the Scrambler of word, The Witch of the Mountains.

"Many years ago, longer than anyone remembers she came to the land of letters looking to take control. The letters and words at first welcomed her; she had not used force and promised much change and prosperity. They let her rule and followed her laws until, one day; someone pointed out that the words were becoming less and less in numbers.

The good people of Diction Land rose up against her and a massive battle was fought, she had her followers, those letters that agreed with her policies. For many years the civil war commenced before she was forced back over the mountains.

As she fled she turned to the advancing army of Alphas and declared that she would return and have her revenge."

"What was her name when she ruled?" asked Pi.

"According to the books she was known as Queen Mannarag."

Z reached across the table and turned over several page of the book lying in front of Ben until he reached a page entitled 'Queen Mannarag.'

Ben felt his curiosity rise up from deep within himself. There is a puzzle here, he thought, and it involves her real name. Ben knew that to save the Alphas, and save adder, he had to figure out how to stop Mannarag and this starts by stopping the Raid Pestgin, he looked over at Z.

He looked down at the book and read the page:
Mannarag from yonder mountain came with powers of the wind and rain,
And fire throwing and lighting seed, in these parts she decreed.
She used these skills to defend her realm and protect her subjects all as well,
And so to rank of Queen they made her seeing her as their good saviour.
Her pale beauty calm and serene, her long flowing hair of emerald green,
Her eyes as blue as blue could be, she ruled for days one hundred & three,
Then she started her plan of babble, of reading words she made unable.
So that people read & write no more, until these lands are gone for sure.
The old man with first armies he led, to take on her with stare of dread,
And forced her back from whence she came, then all the words they rearranged.

Order returned and colourful, Take heed the warning or be the fool.

"There's one thing I don't understand," Ben directed his question as Z, "If she can control the weather and throw fireballs, why does she mix up the words, why not just blow everything up?"

Z sat back in his chair, "The only way to destroy language is to stop people using it. If words become unreadable then no one will read them and language becomes useless and it dies."

The boy sat in silence for a moment; the Queen had powers like nothing he'd seen in this world before. The idea of facing someone who could control the weather and throw balls of fire made him feel somewhat inadequate. And if this Mannarag had captured Adder his life was very much in danger. But where is she? Ben thought, And what is her real name?

With all these question running around in his head Ben wasn't sure where to start trying to find the answers. What would Holmes do? He thought to himself.

Ben had recently acquired a number of Sherlock Holmes novels from a car boot sale at Galedyke Farm. He had gone there with his parents one Sunday morning, the weather was nice and a couple of hours browsing through other people's unwanted items seemed like a fun idea.

He had taken five pounds from the washed out syrup tin he used to keep his birthday money and other change in, just in case he saw something he liked. After about half an hour rummaging through old toys, videos and kitchen gadgets Ben spotted his prize, a complete collection of Sir Arthur Conan Doyle's most famous detective books.

The dog-eared covers enabled Ben to purchase the set for two pounds, a price he was more than happy with. And that afternoon, in the comfort of his bedroom, Ben read how Holmes and Watson unravelled the secret of The Hound of the Baskervilles.

Now, with his own investigation to conduct, Ben thought back to what

Holmes would do. 'Start at the beginning' he imagined the detective saying, 'look for clues.'

"Where was the first village to report problems?" Ben asked Z.

"Well," Z replied to Ben's request, "the first place to report anything was the village of Noun.'"

"Then," said Ben, "It is to the village of Noun we must go."

He stood up from his chair and, holding his hands behind his back, began to pace up and down the office.

"We're going to need a team," he said, "a guide to get us to the village and some guards in case we run into trouble."

"Trouble!" Pi said showing concern, "I don't like the sound of that."

"My dear, Pi," Ben replied, taking on the persona of his literary hero, "we must prepare ourselves for every eventuality."

Z agreed to help assemble a team to escort Ben and Pi to Noun.

"Though it won't be easy," he said, "in light of what happened to Adder and his patrol and the stories guardsman G has been telling, it's going to be hard to get anyone to go."

Ben stopped pacing and turned to look at the leader of letters. Hard did not concern him. Finding Adder did. Hearing the great Z speak with such defeat in his tone angered Ben.

"It is not time to give up yet." He said, "We can still solve this puzzle."

"What puzzle?" replied Z.

Pi nodded in agreement with Z's question.

"From my understanding of mathamagic," Ben said returning to his seat, "You must use the correct name of the object you are trying to effect."

Z sat back in his chair, "It is the same with Word Spells."

"Mannarag is not her real name," Ben paused as he thought, then spoke words that gave the leader new hope in victory, "If we can find her real name then she can be stopped and all the lands surrounding Alphabet City can be saved."

Z stood up, lifting his frame with a renewed vigour. This young boy who sat before him had given him hope and that was all he needed. With only two words, "follow me," he marched with purpose out of the office.

Ben was the first to follow with Pi bringing up the rear. They walked briskly without word through the many corridors of the building. After turning this way and that they eventually arrived at a door. Z placed his hand on the handle and without knocking, swung it open.

The room was very much like the teachers' restroom back at Cottomwall Grammar, only instead of fully dressed adults lounging around on the soft furnishings, there were punctuation marks.

A light green comma was the first to greet them, after a short pause the others followed suit.

Z addressed the entire room with an air of authority, "We need a guide to take these two to Noun."

"Why?" asked a faded yellow question mark stood at the back.

"There could be many reasons," said what looked to Ben like one full stop above another, "They could be: sightseeing, surveying the land or looking for something."

"Three very good suggestion, Colon," said a single full stop to the double vertical dots, "that should be an end to the subject."

Ben was beginning to get confused, he knew what all these punctuation marks were but was getting lost in what they were talking about.

"Hang on," he said holding his hands out in front of him, "all we want is someone to take us to Noun our reasons are our own."

"DON'T MIND THIS LOT!" shouted a light blue exclamation mark who was stood by the window, "LIKE THE REST OF THE CITY THEY HAVE BECOME CAUGHT UP IN THEIR OWN PURPOSE SINCE EVERYTHING STARTED TO FADE!"

"Why are you shouting?" asked Ben.

"Oh he does that all the time," replied Z, "it's what he does."

"THAT'S ME!"

Ben thought tact was in order, "Well can you explain things more quietly?"

The Exclamation Mark thought for a second, he'd never been asked that before.

"Yes!" he said abruptly but much softer, "I think I can!"

Pi was very unsure they were in the right place, to him everyone here had gone completely mad. Ben smiled at the tall upside-down teardrop shape with a perfectly round spot underneath it.

"Do you know the way to Noun?"

The Exclamation Mark walked over to the group, "Yes! Yes I do!"

"Good!" said Z sounding like Exclamation Mark only with a deeper voice, "Then come with us."

Z turned and left the room followed by Pi. Ben stuck out his right hand to the punctuation mark in a gesture of friendship.

"I'm Ben," he said, "and what should I call you?"

"Just call me Exclaim!" he said bluntly shaking Ben's hand.

Ben smiled then followed the other two through the exit. Once in the corridor the left right left journey started again. Ben was amazed that anyone could possibly know where they going through such a labyrinth. He kept looking back to make sure Exclaim was still with them. Keeping pace the punctuation mark that emphasises a sentence bounded up behind them.

Their journey took them through many doors until the last one pushed open to a courtyard. The cold air hit Ben and chilled him to the bone. The courtyard was full of guardsmen marching up and down, turning in unison by the command of an upper-case light blue T. He must be their drill sergeant, thought Ben.

Z walked up to the T and spoke to him, from the distance the other three were standing Ben couldn't make out what was being said. The commands that the T then gave told the boy the answer to the question.

"Company halt!" T shouted with a screech to his voice at the end of every sentence, "Privates C, E and I step forward!"

From deep within the ranks three light green letters emerged. First out was an upper-case I followed closely by a capital E.

The C finally made its way to the front but only after a bit of pushing and shoving, he was much wider than the other two and had a bit of trouble getting past the other letter that were stood to attention. Once they had all taken up their position at the front of the parade the sergeant gave his orders.

"You three are now in the command of Capital Z. C, E and I," the three letters twitched, "wait for it, wait for it!" the sergeant paused, "fall out!"

With that the letters turned sharply ninety degrees right, slammed their left foot hard onto the ground then walked over to Z. The leader of the letters turned fully around and walked back over to the group.

"You have your guide master Ben," Z gestured to the letters that had followed him across the courtyard, "and these are your guards."

Ben looked quizzically at Z, "are you not coming with us?"

"I have to stay here and try to maintain some sort of order."

"I think I should stay too," said Pi.

"What?" asked Ben slightly shocked, "why?"

"I'll only slow you down."

The old symbol placed a hand on Ben's shoulder; Ben smiled and agreed. He knew that Pi wasn't the adventurous type, he fully expected Adder to just be here in the city and didn't for one moment think he would be off looking for witches and monsters.

Ben patted Pi on the shoulder in the same way.

"I shall bring Adder back," he said as comfortingly as he could, "You see if I don't."

"And I'll be here waiting." Pi handed Ben a small glass ball that looked like a clear marble. "I'll call for the Ohm guards to come and help reinforce the city, when you need us, use this."

"How does it work?" Ben asked taking the glass bead.

"You'll know when the time comes."

Z stepped forward, "You'd best be making tracks before the sun goes down."

"The quickest way will be via the river!" said Exclaim in his usual way, "this way!"

He walked off across the courtyard away from the building towards a gate on the other side. Ben started to follow; he turned back to see the letter and the symbol waving. Z said something to the guardsmen, immediately the three of them turned and followed Ben across the parade ground. As the C, E and I came close Ben turned to follow Exclaim. The punctuation mark had already opened the gate and was waiting for the rest to catch up.

To the sounds of marching guards slamming their feet hard onto the ground Ben, the three guardsmen and the exclamation mark, left the city and started their journey to the village of Noun, and hopefully some clues as to the whereabouts of the Mannarag, the Raid Pestgin and Adder.

Chapter MN

Outside the city walls the surrounding countryside was lush and full of the colours that should accompany a forest in the height of summer. The trees were full of green leaves with strong brown trunks. But the cold, that felt wrong. Ben know this was unnatural.

He followed Exclaim down a well trodden path leading through the undergrowth, the guards with their left, right, left right left, marched on behind. After a short walk the group emerged on the bank of a river. The water was so still it looked like a sheet of glass that you could walk on.

A stake, hammered deep into the ground on the bank, sported a rope, which in turn held onto a long boat with low sides. Exclaim boarded the vessel, as he did the boat rocked with his motion causing ripples to spread out across the water. Ben was taught to be polite so offered the guards to board the boat ahead of him.

C waited for Exclaim to take his seat before stepping off the bank; the same rocking and ripples followed. I then stepped forward.

"Hang on there I," said E pulling his colleague back, "If C goes first, I'm next."

"Sorry," replied I, "I forgot."

Ben remembered the rule I before E except after C and chuckled to himself. This should be a fun trip, he thought. Once the two remaining letters had boarded, in the correct order. Ben stepped forward, untied the rope and entered the boat. As with everyone else the boat rocked and Ben had to hold his arms out to keep balance. Once he was happy that he was steady, he sat down.

"Right!" said Exclaim passing forward paddles so that everyone had one, "two on the left and two on the right, that should keep us straight! I'll use the last oar to steer!"

Ben and C said they'd take the right hand side leaving I and E to take care of the left. Being as the riverbank was on their side Ben and C used their paddles to push the boat off and out into the middle of the water.

The first attempt at making the boat move down river failed miserably, all the rowers started dipping their oars in and out of the water with no coordination. E and I kept hitting each other's paddles, while Ben's efforts were counter-actioned by C pulling his oar through the water in the wrong direction. All Exclaim did was shout "No!" and, "Not like that!"

Eventually Ben got fed up.

"Everybody stop!" he commanded. This they did immediately.

"Right," he said, "we'll do this by the numbers. When we hear the number one we all put our oars in the water so that our hands are towards the front of the boat. On two we pull our oars through the water leaning our bodies towards the back. At three we all take our oars out of the water and return it to the position ready for one again."

Ben had learnt this method on one of his camping trips with Stephen. They had taken an inflatable dinghy with them to the Hampton Forest near Cottomwall so they could row down the River Ward to the Merrywitch Falls and have a picnic.

C, E, I and Exclaim agreed that Ben's idea was by far the best way to move forward. Ben asked Exclaim if he would do the counting for them. Exclaim agreed and, after checking to make sure everyone was ready, started.

"One!" They all put their oars in the water.

"Two!" The boat moved forward as, in unison, they pulled their paddles through the water.

"Three!" In perfect synchronicity they all lifted their oars back out of the water and returned them to the starting position.

Slowly the boat cut through the water causing small waves to emanate from the bow and ripple both left and right out towards the riverbanks. The sound of the water being dispersed in time with Exclaim calling out his One, Two, Three's broke the serenity of this tranquil place. Ben felt a little uneasy because of the surrounding silence. No animal noises, he thought, not even birds twittering in the trees.

They had been rowing around the twists and turns of the river for about half an hour when Ben noticed a small wooden pier protruding from the left-hand bank. He pointed this out to Exclaim.

"Yes that's it!" the punctuation mark replied.

The group manoeuvred the vessel over to the docking station with much fuss. The timing they had been using to go in a straight line turned into Exclaim saying, "No back a bit!" and "More on the left!"

The resulting chaos finally got the boat to stop by the pier but only after E, who had been sat behind I, was soaked by the splashing created by I's desperate attempt to follow Exclaims orders.

The wet letter was first out of the boat and, dripping onto the wooden surface of the pier, caught the rope Ben threw over from the bow and tied it to one of the poles that flanked the decking.

"Oi!" said I, "it was my turn to go first."

"Sorry," said E, extending his hand to help his fellow guardsman out onto dry land.

Exclaim was the next to mount the pier followed by C then, with a bit of a wobble, Ben. Exclaim strode down the pier to the riverbank then stopped to get his bearings. E wiped the excess water off himself before following I towards the land, C gestured for Ben to follow on first; the boy nodded his head in thanks before accepting the invitation. As the last two of the group caught up with the others Exclaim was pointing down another well-trodden track that ran away from the river and off to the right.

"This way!" he said advancing down the path.

abcdefghijklmnopqrstuvwxyz

Not knowing where they were the rest of the party accepted this as being the correct direction and followed.

They had walked for around ten minutes before the trees opened up to reveal a village. Like the city all the buildings were grey, unlike the city its occupant were also void of colour.

What seemed like random groups of letters went about their business though instead of looking as if they had any enthusiasm about their given tasks, they all slumped about, hunched over looking depressed.

The party walked slowly towards a group of letters stood on the corner of a street. The letters were arranged in a way that looked like they should be together only the word 'Tampson' made no sense to Ben or any of the others. It wore a sack full to brim with letters over its right shoulder. The sign above its head protruding from what looked like a shop read 'Ice Off Spot'.

"Excuse me?" Ben said to Tampson, "Can you please tell me if we are in Noun?"

Tampson turned to look at the boy, "Yes you are," he said in a most miserable voice, "well it used to be."

Ben was curious, "Are you delivering letters?"

"I suppose so," said Tampson, "But there's no use, since all the words got jumbled up no one can read them."

Ben gazed around the village; all the letters made up words that didn't make any sense.

"Why is everybody so sad?" he asked.

"You'd be sad if you didn't know who you were anymore." Tampson said with a deep sigh, "since the parcel was opened all the names make no sense, the Nouns of Noun are no longer the names of the things that they should be, and no one remembers what they were."

Ben now understood why everyone was so upset; this must have been the

74

work of Mannarag. Ben figured they had to speak to the village leaders and took an educated guess as to whom that might be.

"Can you point us in the direction of the Proper Nouns?"

"Yeah sure," Tampson pointed over to a small round building in the middle of the village, "But they're not Proper Nouns anymore, just another bunch of meaningless letters."

Ben thanked Tampson for his help and sympathised with him for his troubles. This Mannarag has a lot to answer for, he thought beckoning the others over in the direction of the round grey build he had been pointed towards.

The five party members walked across the road, checking for traffic as they did, and knocked on the door. A very sad looking Noty answered.

"Can I help you?" he said in a dull monotone voice.

"Maybe," replied Ben, "we would like to talk to you about what happened here? We think we can help."

Noty stepped back and to one side giving enough room for the group to enter.

"You'd better come in then."

The building was one big circular room with a large round table situated in the centre. Around the outside of the table ten chairs were placed, though only two were currently occupied and one was pulled out from its position of being tucked under the table. Ben figured that Noty must have been sat there.

A bunch of letters making up the word Cluy and another group spelling Linco, neither of whom look remotely interested in the guests that had just arrived, sat in the two taken seats.

"Please have a seat," said Noty as he walked round the table back to his chair.

"Can you tell me what happened here?" asked Ben once sat at the table, "Was this Mannarag?"

"Don't mention her name here!" Cluy said, her voice filled with anger, "Yes it was she that did this, she that took away our names so that we are no longer Proper Nouns."

Linco stood up, "She sent us a gift."

"Yeah some gift!" snapped Cluy.

"Let him speak," Noty said shaking his head.

"A gift," Linco continued, "only, when we opened it instead of the nice surprise we were promised, it unleashed a spell so horrible I can hardly begin to tell…"

Linco started to cry with big heavy sobs. Ben felt very sorry for him, and for everyone else in the village of Noun.

"And it's not just us," said Cluy, "the Verbs got hit by the same trick and now they can't do anything anymore, and I can't even begin to describe what happened to the Adjectives."

"So all the words are gone?" Ben said shocked.

"With the same nasty horrible unmentionable spell," declared Noty.

Exclaim stood up from his seat having become very impatient with the way the conversation was going.

"Well, if we don't know what the spell is we can't even begin to help!"

Cluy slammed her hand on the table, "You don't understand." She paused, it was obvious that she and the others were terrified, "The mixer of words is back and as long as we are in her thoughts we can never be normal again!"

An idea started to form in Ben's mind. Could it be? He thought, If Mathemagical spells work with the rules of maths then maybe word magic…?

He leaned forward and rested his arms on the tabletop.

"Was it an Anagram spell?"

The three former Proper Nouns sat back in their chairs visibly shocked by what Ben had just said.

"Don't say that word!" shrieked Cluy.

"Fancy you knowing that!" cried Exclaim.

"Elementary, my dear Exclaim," Ben had once again become the great detective. "These are not just bunches of random letters but words that have been scrambled, anagrams."

The three scrambled words made more noises of fear. Ben took on a serious expression before qualifying his thoughts with his next question.

"You said as long as you are in her thoughts, what does that mean?"

Noty answered, "Mannarag hates reading and hates words. She said so in her letter."

"What letter?" Ben felt this could be the clue he was looking for, "Bring it here, I must see it."

Linco stood up from the table and walked over to a small cupboard situated just behind the three scrambled words. Inside was a small dark grey safe with a dial mounted in the centre of the door. Linco rotated the dial left, right then left again. With a clunk, he pulled the door open, retrieved a piece of paper from within and carried it around the table to where Ben and his party were sitting.

Ben picked up the note and read:

Dear Nouns,

I cast upon you Nouns and all,

A spell to start this land's downfall.

Anagram all Nouns and Pro I said,

Mix up these words as not to be read.

Kind regards

Queen Mannarag

"So, word spells rhyme," Ben said to himself under his breath.

"The only way to break the spell," Noty said breaking the silence, "Is to destroy Mannarag so that she can't think of us words anymore."

"And she'll not stop at us words," Linco continued, "she won't be satisfied until all the colour has been drained out of language."

Ben was puzzled, "Why would she want to remove all the colour from language?"

"If language has no colour," explained Cluy, "Nobody will read, and if that happens everything in these lands will be gone."

Ben stood up and was just about to insist that this was not an option and he would not rest until this evil Queen was destroyed, when something diverted his attention.

He wasn't sure but to him it felt like a deep rumble through the ground. He signalled to everyone to be still.

"What a loud noise!" cried Exclaim.

Ben held the index finger of his right hand to his lips, "Shhhhh!"

There it was again, only this time the others in the room felt it as well.

"What is that?" asked I who, along with the other guards had been silent all through the conversations.

Just then someone shouted from outside, the call struck fear into all that heard it, including Ben. He knew that at some point this battle would have to be fought only now it was upon him, he wished it would have come later. The shouting increased in volume as more and more yelled out the same warning.

"RAID PESTGIN!"

Ben commanded the guards to follow him as he jumped up out of his chair and ran for the door. Outside the street was full of jumbled up words shouting as they ran in the direction of the river; Ben turned his attention to the end of the village that they were all running from.

The booming thuds and sounds of snapping trees Ben remembered from his dream echoed from the woodland. Mustering up all his bravery Ben started to make his way against the crowd.

"Sir," shouted C, "I think we should be following the others."

"Come on!" he shouted back, waving his arm the urge them on.

Nervously the guards followed. At the end of the street, where the tree line stopped and the buildings began, Ben stood waiting, watching the large shadow thunder its way towards them. The guards started to back up as the sound got closer and closer.

"Hold your nerve!" Ben commanded, as much to himself as the guards behind him.

With an almighty CRACK and CRUNCH the trees at the edge of the forest fell left and right and there, towering over the small boy from earth who had just come looking for his friend was the Raid Pestgin.

Eight thick black legs with hard wire-like hairs supporting a huge body that was made up of two parts. The back section was enormous and round, black with a dark red zig-zag pattern running on the top, this was attached to hard flat black torso, both parts covered in the same wiry hair. At the front of the torso, and causing great concern to Ben were two massive fangs underneath the Raid Pestgins round black eyes.

Ratio spell, Ben thought, quickly calculating a ratio in his head that would make this monster as small as possible. He held his right hand out in front of him, spreading his fingers.

"One to one thousand, one thousand to one, reduce the Raid Pestgin by this ratio!"

He closed his eyes for dramatic effect; the booming thump stopped. Ben slowly opened his eyes and to his horror discovered that the silence wasn't due to the shrinking of the creature, but due to the fact the Raid Pestgin had just stopped moving.

He said the spell again, only this time much, much louder and with his eyes wide open.

"ONE TO ONE THOUSAND, ONE THOUSAND TO ONE, REDUCE THE RAID PESTGIN BY THIS RATIO!"

A sickening feeling formed in the pit of Ben's stomach as he realised that the spell had not worked. Something was very wrong here but instead of turning and running on his heels he was frozen to the spot. Fear had taken control of his muscles and for a moment all he could do was stand there.

The bulbous rear of the Raid Pestgin dropped down and swung through its legs so that the very back was now pointed directly at Ben. He turned to the guards.

"RUN!"

The guards followed this order without hesitation.

A line of sticky web fired from the back of the creature and stuck to Ben's outstretched hand. He turned his head back to see what had just hit him. Seeing the sticky silk over his hand Ben tried to spread out his fingers, but the web was too strong. Shulp! Another line of web was fired, this time it wrapped around Ben's body fixing his other arm to his side. Shulp, Shulp!

Every part of Ben, except his head, was now covered in web. With a jerk, the lines that now entrapped him were lifted by the front left leg of the Raid

Pestgin and attached it to the underside of its torso. With Ben swinging in his webbed prison the creature turned and headed back into the forest.

"BEN!" shouted Exclaim as the monster disappeared off through the forest and into the distance.

Chapter OP

Swinging left and right, forward and back, Ben watched as the forest passed by at some speed. The sound of falling trees accompanied them at every turn. Apart from being suspended from the underneath of the Raid Pestgin; Ben had no idea where he was. The creature darted this way and that causing the cocoon to spin and twist. Ben felt quite sick.

This hadn't been the plan, the ratio spell was supposed to shrink the monster and enable Ben to capture it himself. He couldn't understand why it didn't work; he'd gotten his sums right of that he was sure, and he got the words right with the exact name and everything. Maybe, he thought, Mathemagical spells don't work here?

It felt like hours before things changed, the creature slowed and Ben could see from the ground that they had come out of the forest, the grey hard rocks told him they were at the foot of the mountains. Ben felt strange as the world around him turned on its side. The Raid Pestgin was climbing up the side of a cliff face. Ben shut his eyes; he was scared enough as it was and seeing how high they were going wouldn't help matters.

Before long Ben could feel that the monster had climbed over the top of the cliff and was once again on horizontal land, but before he could open his eyes he had the sudden sensation of falling followed very quickly by a bump! He opened his eyes to find himself lying on the ground. The enormous figure of the Raid Pestgin moved slowly away to the right and with it went the shade.

The bright sunlight hurt Ben's eyes and it took him a moment to get his bearings. The creature that had brought him here walked over to the mouth of a cave, turned around, then backed into the rocky opening until only the tips of its front two legs were showing.

The area Ben was lying in was like the entrance to a great palace carved out of the very mountain itself. To his right was the cave the Raid Pestgin had just retired to, and on his left a small door made of stone. Directly opposite the cliff's edge was an amazingly ornate entrance with tall thin carvings of dragons guarding each side of the two stone doors. The entire arch looked bigger than the gates of Alphabet City.

A small thing opened the door to Ben's left. It looked like a small green blob about half Ben's size. It had arms and legs but no real body to speak of; it was like a hairless head with limbs.

The thing skipped over the where Ben was lying and spoke with a slimy nasally voice.

"It's the boy," it said to itself before shouting over to the door.

"It's the BOY!"

Another green blob only much fatter than the first one, appeared at the small entrance. It looked around as if checking the coast was clear then skipped, but not as freely, over to the same spot.

"You see," said the first blob, "Mistress will be pleased."

"Oh yes," said the second with a similar voice to the first only with a slightly deeper tone, "Mistress will be very pleased."

The two blobs clasped hands and started jumping and swung each other around in some strange childish dance while singing, "Mistress will be pleased, Mistress will be pleased."

"Excuse me!" shouted Ben, now fed up of not being able to move and becoming irritated by the moronic singing and dancing, "Can you please stop playing and untie me?"

The two blobs instantly stop prancing about and looked over at Ben with expressions of deep disappointment.

"Did you hear that Numpty?" said the first one.

"Yes I did." Replied Numpty, "The boy wants to be untied. What do we say to that Numskull?"

Numpty and Numbskull smiled at each other then, with one almighty leap landed next to Ben, leaned over him and blew the biggest raspberries Ben had ever heard into his face covering him with spit. Ben shook his head with utter disgust in a feeble attempt to remove the blob of saliva.

"Come on Numpty," said Numbskull grabbing hold of Ben's wrapped up legs.

"Righty Ho, Numbskull," replied Numpty also getting a grip of the boy's legs.

With a heave and the sound of Ben's protests, Numbskull and Numpty dragged the poor unfortunate child across the floor and in through the small entrance.

Once the door slammed shut darkness fell. It took Ben several minutes for his eyes to adjust to the gloom. In this time he was pulled this way and that, dragged down cold wet corridors made of damp smelling stone. By the time he could see a bit better the two blobs stopped, then with a big key, unlocked a door. The sound of grinding metal echoed round the stone as the rusty hinges were forced to move.

Inside Ben could see two cages and one very secure looking wooden box. Numpty picked up a lump of rock with a sharp edge and proceeded to cut the web from around Ben's body. Once he felt free Ben tried to escape by running to the door.

"Oh no you don't!" said Numbskull grabbing hold of the strap of Ben's shoulder bag .

The blob yanked Ben back with such force that he couldn't keep his feet. With a trip and a fall Ben flew headlong into the cage Numpty had just opened. The door to the cage was slammed shut. The key, which had been hung on a metal ring with some others, was rattled in the lock and Ben was prisoner.

The two blobs hung the keys on a hook just to the left of the room door then, singing about how happy the Mistress was going to be, closed and locked it behind them.

Q q

R r

Chapter QR

As the singing faded into the distance of the dark, damp tunnels of this mountain palace Ben sighed, the light wasn't good enough to see and in his cold, dark cell; Ben felt ever so alone.

"Oh Adder!" he said breathing out another very big sigh.

"Yeth," came a hissing voice from within the wooden box. "Ben, is that you?"

"ADDER!" Ben leaped up with the delight of hearing his friends voice only, he didn't realise the cage was so small and banged his head hard against the bars.

"Watch those cages Ben," hissed Adder, "they're a bit small. "

"Oh Adder," Ben said rubbing his head; he was sure there was the start of a big bump forming, "it's so good to hear your voice."

Ben removed the bag from his shoulder and rummaged around in it. There were certain items Ben always kept in his bag; a torch; a small hand towel and a Manchester City scarf his Gran had bought him from Ashton market during one of his visits. He located the torch, pulled it out and switched it on.

The room was illuminated by the glow of his torch. On the other side of the wooden box Ben could see the other cage. Sat in the corner with his knees bent and his arms wrapped round them was an old man with long grey hair and a very long grey beard.

"Oh, hello sir," Ben said seeing that he and Adder were not alone.

"Ben," said Adder poking his head out of a small hole in the top of the box, "I'd like you to meet Mr Richard Lexiur. Mr Lexiur, this is Ben Small."

"Nice to make your acquaintance," croaked the old man.

"Likewise," reciprocated Ben.

Ben looked up at the snake, "Adder it's great to see you, but we have to get out of here. The colour has already gone from the words, and the people of Alphabet City look a bit pale."

"I agree," said Adder nodding his head, "but the keys are over by the door, the bars are too strong to bend, and this is the only hole in this box," he strained to try and push himself through the hole his head was sticking out of, "and this hole is too tight for me to get through."

Ben placed his torch on the floor of the cage, balancing it in such a way so it still lit the room. He grabbed hold of the bars that made up the door of his cell. With frustration hanging heavy on him, he rattled the locked gateway so hard the jangling must have been heard all through the palace.

Ben imagined Numpty and Numbskull laughing at the sound of his futile attempt to force the cell door open. He sat down and kicked his legs out knocking his bag into the torch moving the light from pointing at the ceiling to firing directly at the wall. For a second Ben felt angry at the fact that the bag he had kicked had just knocked over the torch, then he smiled.

He scrambled forward grabbing his bag and frantically opened it up.

"What are you doing Ben?" enquired Adder.

"I have an idea!"

Ben pulled all his books, pens, pencils and his hand towel out, discarding them with no thought as to where they were landing. There rolled up in the bottom of his satchel was the item he wanted; his Manchester City scarf.

He withdrew it from his bag and, with a look of sheer excitement, showed it to Adder. Now Ben knew what he was intending to do with his coveted sky blue and white neck warmer. However, his assumption that Adder would also know what he intended was quite utterly proved wrong by Adder's next statement.

"Good idea Ben, you must keep warm."

Ben sighed, tilted his head slightly to the right then responded, abcdefghijklmnop**qr**stuvwxyz

"No Adder," he said like a parent explaining to a child why covering yourself in flour when making a cake was not a good idea, "I'm going to use this to get the keys."

Adder looked confused.

The Manchester City scarf Ben's Gran had purchased for him from Ashton market was different from most other scarves for a number of reasons. First it was very cheap, his Gran didn't have a lot of money and hunting for bargains was a skill she had acquired over many years rummaging in the right places all over Manchester. Secondly the reason it was so cheap was due to the fact that it wasn't quite right; it had a couple of manufacturing faults. The football club's crest was the wrong way round and the machine that made it had gone a bit mad and didn't stop when it was supposed to. The result was a scarf three times longer than it should have been.

Ben didn't mind, he loved the scarf because it was his team and his Gran had bought it for him. Because wearing it wasn't wise due to its length, Ben kept it in his bag. Now he had an idea to use it like a rope to retrieve the keys from their resting-place on the hook by the door of the room.

He tied a big knot in one end, this was to make it heavier so he could get a good throw. It also provided a large solid end to try and knock the keys to the floor. After this he tied the other end to one of the bars of the cage. This was to stop him losing the scarf should, after a big throw, it slip out of his hands, thus losing the scarf altogether to the other side of the room.

Ben moved himself to the edge of the cage, placed his arms through the bars and picked up the solid knotted end of the scarf ready for his first throw. Adder and Richard watched intensely.

With a swift underarm action Ben launched the woollen projectile. The snake and the old man followed the fight path, their heads moving up, along, then down as the knot fell short of its target and bounced on the floor.

Ben tugged the scarf back in and readied himself to try again. This time he gave it a bit more oomph. The knot sailed up through the air then down right on top of the keys, causing them to jangle and shift on the hook, but not drop.

"Unlucky lad," said Richard, getting quite excited by the game afoot.

Adder pitched in his wisdom, "Try and hit them on the underside."

Ben glanced over at the snake, nodding his head to indicate he had taken the advice onboard. In order to strike the keys as Adder had suggested Ben had to throw from a lower position and throw straighter, not so up and down.

He lined himself up with the target, rested his knuckles on the ground then, closing his eyes in an attempt to get more power, hurled the knot. This time it went very straight and very fast, smashing into the keys below the hook. The impact threw them upward over the hook and set them free to fly off into the room somewhere.

The extra effort Ben had put into the throw had caused him to bang his nose on the bars of his cage. He shook his head and rubbed his sore snout.

"Did I get them?" he said rather nasally.

Richard was like a young man again, "You sure did lad," he hadn't had this much fun in years, "great shot!"

"Where did they go?" asked Adder.

Ben picked up his torch and scanned the room. In front of Richard's cage he could see the bunch of keys heaped on the floor.

"There Richard!" said Adder trying to point at them with his head.

Richard reached through the bars but the metal givers-of-freedom were out of reach. He tried stretching further until the bars distorted his face. He strained every muscle in this arm, hands and fingers, just to try and gain that extra millimetre. The large metal ring that held all the keys together brushed faintly against his fingertips, but no matter how much he tried, he just couldn't get hold of them.

Ben recoiled the scarf, took the knot in his right hand, aimed and threw it directly at the keys. With a tinkle of metal on stone the woollen projectile hit the bunch of keys pushing them toward the outstretched hand of Mr Lexiur. Richard's fingers curled round the metal ring and with a quick jerk snatched the keys into his cage.

Ben and Adder gave out a quiet cheer while Richard, who was slightly out of breath from the exertion, fell back and smiled broadly under his beard.

He took a deep breath before setting about the task of finding the key. There were four in total, one for each of the cages, one for the box Adder was held in and one for the door.

The old man figured that the two keys that looked similar would be for the cages. He picked one and tried it, but it wouldn't turn in the lock. He tried the next one, click, Richard was free.

He hurried over to Ben's cage and used the first key he had tried, this time it worked and the cage door swung open. Ben gathered his belongings together and put them back in his bag.

Richard turned his attention the box that held Adder. Out of the two keys he hadn't used he decided that the smaller one would be most likely to remove the big iron padlock that sealed the snake inside. Turning the key in the lock he was proved right. The snake was most grateful to the old man for setting him free.

Ben gave Adder a huge hug; he was so relieved to see his friend again, and alive. Richard walked over to the door to unlock it.

"Wait," said Ben, "we have to formulate a plan."

"I just want to go home," Richard proclaimed turning away from the door to face Ben, "I've been here so long I've forgotten what it looks like."

"How long have you been here?" asked the boy.

"Well lad," he replied, "the queen has been planning this word scramble for years. I was the first one captured, I am too dangerous to her you see."

Adder thought he should explain, "You see Ben, Mr Lexiur is a Word Magician and he has all his spells memorised."

Ben didn't understand why this was dangerous to Mannarag.

Richard took over the story, "The thing is lad, I don't read like everyone else. To me all words are jumbled up."

"Like anagrams," said Ben.

"Yes," replied the old man, "just like anagrams. But when the Queen started jumbling and scrambling-up all the words, to me they read correctly."

"So Mannarag enabled you to read?" Ben's curiosity was getting hold of him.

"And being as magic, word or number, requires the correct name of what you are trying to effect to be used…"

Ben's eyes widened, "You're the only one that knows her real name?"

Richard smiled and nodded.

"So if everything is an anagram," Ben started to recap, "Raid Pestgin isn't the name of the creature?"

"He catches on fast this one," said Richard to Adder.

"I know," replied the snake with a distinct look of pride.

Ben picked up the keys and used one of them to scratch letters on the stone of the floor.

RAIDPESTGIN

"What are you doing?" asked Adder.

Ben looked up, "I'm trying to work out what this anagram is so that the ratio spell will work."

"Well that's easy," said Richard, now looking over Ben's shoulder, "You've written GIANT SPIDER."

98

"Of course!"

Ben scratched more letters underneath the first lot.

GIANT SPIDER

All the letters in Raid Pestgin were also in Giant Spider. *That's why the ratio spell didn't work*, he thought to himself.

He turned his mind to the Queen's name Mannarag. He couldn't figure out any words at all. Then it hit him, It's her name, he thought, But that can't be possible, can it? Ben scratched some more letters onto the floor.

"I think I know the Queens name," he stated.

"You've written Mannarag?" said Richard.

"No," said Adder, "that's not what he's written at all."

Chapter ST

Richard pushed the last of the keys into the lock on the door, turned it to the left until he heard a clunk then slowly pulled the door towards him. A slight breeze whisked in through the opening sending a chill down the spine of all three of them. Ben gave Richard the mirror he had brought from Pi's house to check round the corners. The old man took it in his left hand. First he checked to the right then left.

"It's all clear." He whispered.

Creeping as to make no noise, the freed prisoners left the dank room and entered the corridor. Ben turned to the right.

"This way," he said, "I remember being brought in from the left, so the palace must be this way."

"Well I'm going this way." Richard started to walk in the other direction.

Ben looked shocked, "But we need your help."

"I want to go home," came the solemn reply, "this is not my fight."

Ben stepped forward passed Adder who was standing by the open door, his head turning left then right to watch the one talking.

"If Mannarag succeeds," Ben said with an angry tone, "and the colour is gone from all language…"

"It's nothing to do with me."

"Once the colour has gone people in my world will stop reading…"

"And if that happens," interrupted Adder, "everything in these lands will be destroyed."

Ben looked straight into the old Word Magician's eyes, "Then you won't have a home."

abcdefghijklmnopqrstuvwxyz

Richard looked down at the floor. All he wanted to do was get back to his little house on the outskirts of Diction Land, sit by the large open fireplace with carvings of swans decorating each side, drink a cup of hot chocolate and practise his magic.

What Ben had said made sense, however much he didn't care for the others in the land for calling him names and picking on him for not being able to read like they could, he couldn't see the entire land, or its people wiped out. He took a deep breath.

"Lead on lad."

Ben smiled, so did Adder, they turned and started to move deeper in the underbelly of the palace.

The corridors were damp and cold, mold and mildew crawled their way up the walls leaving in their trail a musky stale smell. Ben considered whether this was what the old castles back in the Middle Ages must have been like.

After a short while they arrived at a T-junction. The light wasn't good enough for Ben to see clearly in either direction and he didn't want to risk using his torch in case someone saw the light.

"This way," whispered Adder with a hiss, pointing his tail to the right, "there are some stairs leading up here."

"I can't see anything," said Ben.

"One of the advantages of being snake," replied Adder. "You can see in the dark."

Adder led the way as the three of them made their way towards the stairs.

"I don't like this," grumbled Richard.

Twenty stone steps led up to a wooden door. The light from the room beyond bust through the gap under the door illuminating the top ten steps. Adder slithered up first followed by Ben who walked on tiptoe. Richard allowed the others to get most of the way up before he started to climb.

Adder kept his head low, when he reached the top he peered through the gap that had been responsible for letting in the light, Ben crouched down to do the same.

The room was full of blob guards sitting around, eating pink slime and laughing out loud, there must have been over a hundred of them. Richard joined his comrades at the top of the stairs, and like the other two, looked through the gap under the door.

"Numpties, Numbskulls and Ninnys," he whispered.

"Ninnys?" questioned Ben.

"Yeah, you see those tall thin ones?" Richard pointed out a tall thin guard, "They're Ninnys."

One of the Ninnys walked past a Numbskull who was sitting with his feet up on a rock. He stumbled knocking the Numbskull's drink over spilling the beaker's brown muddy contents, which looked like dirty river water, into his lap. The Numbskull leapt to his feet furious with the Ninny shouting at the tall thin guard calling him a stupid clumsy oaf. The altercation soon turned into a fight, much to the delight of a number of Ninnys, Numbskulls and Numpties.

"The thing about Queen Mannarag's guards is," said Richard, "they are stupid."

Ben didn't understand, "Why would she surround herself with stupid people?"

Adder looked over to Ben, "Idiots are easy to control, they'll believe anything you tell them."

Ben turned his attention back to the room; the Numbskull whose drink had been spilt was lying on the floor, those onlookers who had taken the side of the Ninny were holding him aloft. The losing supporters were looking somewhat dejected though, they were still cheering the winner. Idiots, thought Ben.

"We need to create a diversion," Adder said scratching his chin with his tail. "Mathemagic will be no use, they're too stupid for numbers."

"And Word Magic won't work either," said Richard twirling his long grey beard with the index finger of his left hand, "I could throw a word search in there but they wouldn't know what to do with it."

Ben thought really hard; he considered just opening the door and telling the guards the Queen had let them go, I don't think they're that stupid, he put the idea out of his head. Then he had the notion of taking one of his school books out of his bag, opening the door a little then throwing it into the corner in order to make a noise. The guards would go and investigate and when they did…

No this idea is more stupid than the guards are. Then it hit him, noise.

"Onomatopoeia," he said out loud to no one in particular.

"What?" said Adder.

"Clever," said Richard.

"I don't understand?" replied Adder creasing his eyebrows into the middle of his head to emphasise this.

It was Ben's turn to be teacher, "An onomatopoeia is a sound word, or a word that is a sound, like whiz or splash."

"Or bang," said Richard.

"Exactly!" confirmed Ben.

"And how will that help?" asked Adder.

"There is an onomatopoeia spell," Richard seemed to gain some interest, "I could cast the bang over by that door." He pointed to a door on to opposite wall, "Once the word is created the guards will go and have a look."

"Then we can get into the room and up those stairs over there." Ben pointed at the stone staircase leading up over on the right.

With no other plan available Adder agreed.

"Let me just think about it a second," said Richard running his right hand through his thick grey hair, "all word spells have to rhyme you see."

His eyes flicked left and right then up and down, his nostrils twitched and his fingers twizzled; Ben could almost hear him think. Suddenly, every microscopic movement made by the old man stopped and he smiled before dipping down again in order to see under the door. He placed his right hand out in front of him, extending the index finger so as to point at the door; his intended target. Then in a dry croaky voice, he cast his spell.

> "Numbskulls, Numpties, Ninnies and all,
> My word of sound In yonder hall,
> Ninnies, Numpties, Numbskulls all hear,
> The word is BANG onomatopoeia!"

No sooner had the last word been uttered than a very loud, hard BANG echoed from behind the door on the opposite wall. The guards immediately stopped what they were doing and looked over to where the sound came from. A very brief moment of stillness followed then, all at once, every Numpty, Numbskull and Ninny ran over to the door.

The first guardsman there, a Numbskull, opened the door, then like a rampaging herd of wild rhinoceros, all the guards charged though and ran down the corridor on the other side.

The fugitives had to move quickly; however stupid the guards were it wouldn't be long before they realised that they had been duped and head back. Richard was the closest to the door handle and turned it.

Quickly but quietly the three moved across the room toward the stairs. They couldn't go in a straight line, more darting left and right to avoid the disgusting mess of the randomly discarded food. The last thing any of them wanted was to get any of that stuff on them.

From down the corridor on the other side of the open door the chaotic noise of the guards could be heard. The three arrived at the bottom of the stairs; another twenty steps climbed up to a wooden door, only this time they were well lit. The three climbed the stairs and peered under the gap at the bottom of the door.

A large room as long as a football pitch, and equally as wide, spread out before their eyes. From this angle they couldn't see how tall it was; the smooth stone walls stretched up out of view. It reminded Ben of the great halls and throne chambers he had seen in the drawings of many of his history books, and like those drawings at the far end was a large ornate throne.

The royal seat looked like it was facing away from them. They could see the legs of it occupant and make out that the seated dignitary was wearing bright red shoes however, by the look of the single leg supporting the throne in the middle of the seat, it looked like it swivelled round like an office chair.

Just then Ben's attention was drawn to the room at the bottom of the stairs, the noise that raged from the other corridor was getting louder.

"They're coming back." He whispered.

Adder and Richard both turned to listen. The boy was right very soon the room would be filled with over a hundred Numpties, Ninnies and Numbskulls, and by the light on these stairs, they would be seen.

"What are we going to do?" Said Richard.

"As I see it we have two choices," said Adder, "Stand and fight or…"

Before he could finish Ben had turned the handle on the door and slowly opened it just enough to get through. He signalled to the others to follow him then, on his hands and knees, crawled in to the throne chamber.

"Was that your other suggestion?" asked Richard.

Adder smiled, "Yes it was."

Richard was the next to crawl through, like Ben he stopped to hold the door open for the next one to creep in. Ben was sat silent with his back against the wall. He hardly wanted to breathe in case he was heard. Adder entered the room and Richard closed the door and sat next to Ben.

It was like being sat in a Cathedral. Four giant stone pillars decorated with carvings of dragons ran down each side of the main polished stone causeway. The ceiling was painted with a massive mural depicting a woman with long green hair blowing wildly behind her. The silver dress she was wearing, which fell all the way down to her red shoes, flowed across the back of the giant spider she rode. Her face wore an expression of rage mixed with enjoyment. Around her and her beast, letters and words ran off in fear as she threw fire at them.

Adder had entered the room but just as he was about to slowly close the door a gust of wind blew up the great hall from the far end. It was just enough to ruffle Ben's hair, cold enough to send a shiver down Richard's spine and strong enough to take control of the closing door from Adder and slam it shut!

BANG!

The sound of the door returning to its position in its frame, at speed, echoed through the chamber, bouncing off the walls and reverberating from the ceiling. The bang repeated several times, getting quieter with each play, before silence fell upon the hall again.

For a moment Ben, Richard and Adder froze. If you'd asked them each would have said that their hearts actually stopped and left their normal place of residence in their chests and journeyed up to their throats.

The throne at the other end of the hall slowly turned on its pivot bringing into view the same woman captured in painting on the ceiling. In her hands she held a small 'and'. The little word squirmed in a vain attempt free itself but the Queen's grip was far too tight. To the horror of the onlookers she physically pulled the letters apart and rearranged them to read nad before tossing it to one side. The scrambled word whimpered as it limped off to hide in a corner of the room.

With grace never before seen by Ben she rose from her seated position, the full length of her hair flowed down to her knees. Her pale lifeless skin exaggerated the redness of her lips. Her long red fingernails, like claws, gave her a fearsome look.

Her completely blue eyes, no white, no colour, no pupil, just solid blue, disturbed Ben. She fixed her stare on the boy, then without moving her lips she spoke to him.

"Come to me." She said using the index finger of her right hand to beckon the boy forward.

Without thought Ben started to walk. He didn't know why but for some reason he just had to do what she said.

"Ben," Adder had the voice of concern, "don't look into her eyes. BEN!"

Adder shouting his name distracted Ben's attention. He suddenly shook his head and looked back at his snake friend. A weird detached feeling, as if he'd just woken from a deep sleep, came over him.

"Ben," echoed Mannarg's voice, cold and hard, "come to me Ben."

Ben could feel himself becoming angry, not only had he been captured, his friend had been locked in a box, the words he loved from his books were being messed up and now this so called Queen had used some sort of hypnotic trance on him.

Now, the worst thing you can ever do is act upon a thought when you are angry. The ability to consider whether or not it's a good idea disappears from you and the chances are that the next action you take will do more harm than good. Ben's Gran knew this and had always told him to count to ten. 'It gives you time to think,' she would say.

Only here Ben forgot what his Gran had told him. Everything was red in his eyes and all he wanted to do was stop Mannarag from doing anymore damage. Richard could see the boy's expression and feared the worst.

"We have to stop him!" he said to Adder, "He mustn't let her wind him up and loose control."

Adder agreed, "Ben!" he said trying to use his most authoritative voice, "You calm down right now."

Ben looked straight into Adder's eyes. He calmed down enough to stop himself doing what he was just about to do, though he didn't say anything. He only stood there.

The door leading to the guard room burst open and the Numpties, Numbskulls and Ninnys flooded into the great hall.

"Wait!" commanded Mannarag.

The guards stopped immediately.

"I think it's time to feed the Raid Pestgin. Lead them outside!"

The three captives were ushered in the direction of the enormous doors. As Ben came up alongside Adder he whispered to him.

"Thank you." Adder just smiled before being pushed forward by a Numpty.

Mannarag marched up the hall to follow the party outside. As the doors opened the cold wind that entered blew through her hair causing it to spread out and dance as if it had a life of its own.

"Come, come," she said clapping her hands together, "my pet must be hungry."

Chapter UV

The sun was on its way down off in the distance throwing long shadows across the courtyard that Ben had been brought to by the Queens pet. The grey stone had an orange hue from the evening sky yet, despite the warmth of the colours the air was still bitter.

Ben, Adder and Richard were forced in the centre then surrounded by the idiot guards. Mannarag strode out and took up a position with her back to the opening that led out towards the cliff and the forest; her black silhouette throwing a long shadow over the condemned.

"Now would be a good time to stop this Mannarag," shouted Adder, "You could still walk away."

Ben was confused why the general of the Mathamagical didn't use her real name. The self-proclaimed Queen just laughed.

"And what are you going to do Snake"

"I warned you years ago…" Adder didn't get a chance to finish.

"And now I'm back!" Her voice became harsh, "You couldn't stop me then and you have failed again."

Ben looked at Adder but the snake wasn't breaking eye contact with the evil Queen. What did he mean years ago? Ben wondered. He realised that there was more to Adder than he knew. He looked over at Richard; the old man was just looking at the floor. Ben felt guilty about dragging him along.

"Enough!" shouted Mannarag, "bring forth the Raid Pestgin!"

Two Numbskulls ran over to the beast's cave, picked up sticks and started poking at the creature.

"Come on my pet," Mannarag said trying to sound sweet. "Din dins."

The enormous frame of the Raid Pestgin rose slowly. The Numbskulls ran back to their ranks and watched with the rest at the fearsome sight as the monstrous creature advanced from the cavern towards the boy, snake and old man.

"What are we to do?" Richard said cowering behind Adder.

Adder turned to Ben, "Use the ratio spell."

"But it didn't work last time?"

"No," said Adder, "but NOW you know its real name."

Ben was suddenly filled with confidence. He turned to face the beast. By now the creature was bearing down upon them. Its jowls, dripping with saliva, opened and closed with a horrible squelching noise. Ben stepped forward and, as before, raised his right hand, spreading his fingers out as if he was commanding it to stop.

"One thousand to one, one to one thousand…"

Mannarag began to laugh a cackling laugh, sharp and evil.

"Shrink this Giant Spider to this ratio!"

The Queen's laugh instantly became silent. The boy knew her pet's real name and in that moment she knew he would also know hers. Her eyes narrowed and her lips tightened.

Before Ben's eyes the once imposing figure of the Raid Pestgin or Giant Spider began to shrink. Within seconds the beast was no bigger and no more dangerous than a common house spider. Fearing for its life the small arachnid made a run for it, scurrying as fast as its now little legs could carry it, back to the safe shadows of the cave.

Ben turned to face Mannarag.

"And now it's your turn Anna Gram!"

Her worst fears were confirmed; they knew her name and that meant magic would work on her. The guards manoeuvred themselves to form a barrier between the Queen and the only three that could now stop her.

Ben did a quick calculation in his head, "Twenty to one, one to twenty…"

Anna lifted up her arms, clasped her hands over her head then with a single quick movement threw something down onto the floor. There was a blinding flash followed by a large amount of pink smoke.

As the smoke cleared Ben could see that Anna Gram had made her escape; she was nowhere to be seen. The guards moved closer together in order to create a tougher barrier to cross.

"Where has she gone?" demanded Adder.

"We have to get past this lot first," said Richard.

Adder slithered forward and raised his tail in front of him, "The number of Ninnies divide by two, round down and show me the answer!"

With this the number of ninnies halved. Ben saw a group of eight of them suddenly become four. Adder repeated the spell; those four Ninnies then became two.

Ben started to repeat the spell only instead of Ninnies he said Numpties. Richard did the same using the word Numbskulls. Very quickly the guards were whittled down to just three; one numbskull, one Numpty and one Ninny.

The last remaining guards looked at each other, turned back to the three friends, back at each other again then ran as fast as they could back into the stone palace.

"I like Mathemagical spells," said Richard nodding at Ben, "they don't have to rhyme."

"Come on," said Adder, "we have to find out where Anna has gone."

"I think I know where she's going," said Richard.

"Where?" asked Adder.

"Palindrome Gorge," replied Richard.

"Of course!" said Adder slapping himself on the forehead with his tail. "How silly of me."

Ben didn't understand what they were talking about, and told them this.

"Palindrome Gorge is a gap in the mountains that looks exactly the same from both ends," explained Richard.

"Like a palindrome word or phrase, that reads the same backwards as it does forwards," confirmed Ben.

"Yes," said Richard, "it leads through to the Snrevac Caverns. If she gets to them we could lose her."

"And in order to correct the effects of her spells," continued Adder, "we have to stop her. If she gets away she could hold the spell over the words and letters forever."

"The quickest way to the gorge is through the forest," Richard said running to the edge of the cliff.

The three of them looked over the edge and down the steep drop.

"Well, she managed it," said Ben.

"Unless she didn't go across the forest," said Richard. "She might have taken the slower mountain path."

Adder raised his head from looking at the drop. "Then we can get to the gorge before her."

"Only if we can get down there," Ben said pointing down.

The drop to the forest floor must have been at least one hundred and eighty metres of sheer rock face; it looked impossible to climb. No equipment, no magic spells that could help and no friendly giant spider to carry them, all seemed lost. They knew they couldn't catch her along the mountain path even if they could find where it started.

"Wait a moment," said Ben having an idea, "We don't have a giant spider, but…"

He stopped mid sentence, turned and walked over to the cave the Raid Pestgin took shelter in; it was dark and cold. Ben took his torch out of his bag and fired the light into the chasm. The now small once-great-spider ran to hide under a rock fearing that the boy had come to finish him off; this was the last thing on Ben's mind. The light from the torch illuminated the contents of the cave; it was exactly what Ben was expecting to see.

Ben had seen a programme on the television about spiders. The documentary spoke about how some of the eight-legged creatures like to live in holes rather than in the middle of a web like the ones you find in a garden. Even though they made their home under a rock or in the ground they still spun a web, creating a cocoon that alerted them to possible food or danger walking by.

The Raid Pestgin was no different. The walls, ceiling and floor were covered in thick sticky web. Adder and Richard moved up alongside the boy.

"Great," said Richard, "Giant cobwebs!"

"No," said Ben. "Very long and very strong rope."

Richard looked at Adder; the snake was smiling broadly. He always enjoyed it when Ben figured out how to get around a problem; it gave him a sense of pride. Ben entered the cave and started to pull the web from the walls; the old man and the General joined in to help.

The web came away from the wall relatively easily. They could feel how strong it was; there was no way this stuff would snap. They kept pulling and pulling and pulling. It was as if the entire cave was covered by one single continuous strand of web.

Eventually they got to an end; one entire wall was now clear as was half the ceiling. Ben looked to the mouth of the cave. The pile of spider rope was massive. That should be enough, he thought.

"Right," he said marching out of the cave, "we need to tie one end to something, close to the edge if possible."

There didn't seem to be anything suitable. All the rocks were too small, there were no trees and no posts. Ben sized up the length of the courtyard from the edge of the cliff to the large double doors of the palace. About   ten metres.

He picked up one end of the web and ran over to the doors. He could tell by the thickness of the strands that these spider spun ropes would easily hold the weight of each member of his party, it was the distance from the edge to the ground he was worried about. What if they didn't have enough to reach all the way down? With no other options available he just had to try.

When the doors were shut the two door handle were side by side in the middle, their design, a loop of metal with a bolt fixing them to the door top and bottom, was perfect for fixing the rope. Ben fed the end through the right hand one first, then through the left making sure he pulled enough of the web through to do the same again and still have enough over to tie a knot. He looped it around five times before securing it with a bowline knot.

Stephen had showed him how to tie this knot on one of their camping trips. To get it right he repeated the phrase his stepfather had taught him.

"The rabbit comes out of its hole, round the tree and back down the hole again"

Ben then tugged at the web to make sure the knot wasn't slipping. Once he was happy that it wasn't going to open back up he ran back to the pile to find the other end. Adder and Richard had already dug it out from the bottom and were busily checking the rest of the line to make certain it was tangle free.

Ben picked up the loose end and ran over to the edge of the cliff. With a big heave he hurled it over and watched it drop. The weight of the web still in the courtyard held the falling rope back but with a bit of assistance from Ben and his party the rope was soon falling at some speed.

The pile rapidly reduced in size growing smaller and smaller as the descending rope headed towards the foot of the cliff. Before long the pile was gone and the web suddenly stopped moving. Ben peered over the edge; the rope hadn't quite reached the bottom but from where he was standing it looked almost there with just a short drop at the end.

abcdefghijklmnopqrstuvwxyz

"I'll go first," proclaimed Adder.

He slithered up to the cliff's edge. Because of the height of the door handles the rope was lifted off the ground. Adder twirled himself round the cord wrapping around it three times; with no arms or legs this was the only way he knew to climb ropes. Ben and Richard helped the snake get over the sharp edge then, whoosh, he was off, head first down the side of the cliff. The rope pulled tight against the door handles causing the large wooden barriers to knock against their frames.

Richard was next, he claimed to have done this sort of thing before. The old man picked up the spider-spun rope and held it tight. Then he leaned backwards over the edge allowing the fixing to take his weight. The stickiness of the web helped with the grip. Slowly, he started to walk backwards down the cliff feeding the rope through his hands as he did.

"For an old man he's pretty agile," Ben said to himself, "and if he can do it, so can I."

Ben took the rope in the same way Richard had, his heart beating hard against his chest. Slowly he allowed himself to fall back and breathing deep he started his descent.

Walking one hundred and eighty metres wouldn't normally take very long, but when you're walking backwards, holding onto a rope and trying not to slip, travelling that distance takes much longer.

Adder was already on the ground with Richard when Ben got to the end of the hanging web. The drop from the bottom of the rope to the floor was only about four metres so it didn't pose much of a problem. Ben allowed himself to hang at the end of the rope, waited until it stopped swinging, then dropped.

He looked back up the cliff face before turning his attention to the forest. Richard took the lead followed by Ben, Adder bringing up the rear. The three wasted no more time; as fast as they could they made their way deep into the woodlands.

Ben caught up with Richard and walked beside him. He was curious as to what you could do with Word Magic.

"Well," began Richard, "you can do anything words can."

"But words can do so many things," said Ben.

"And so can Word Magic." The old man rifled through his brain for examples, "When you're first learning you get to create colours, sounds and puzzles."

"Puzzles?"

"You know," Richard explained, "word searches, that sort of thing."

"Oh," Ben understood.

Richard continued, "More powerful Word Wizards can create whole worlds just by using the power of description."

Ben was fascinated and asked Richard to show him how to create a Word Search.

"A Word Search is a grid with a number of words hidden amongst random letters." Richard teacher voice was back, "So you cast your spell by saying how many letters wide by how many letters deep you want your grid. Then you say how many words you want hidden and so on. Here I'll show you one."

Richard stopped walking and looked at Ben.

"For Ben to see

And words to read

About birds and plants

Make this for me.

Read horizontal vertical and diagonally

abcdefghijklmnopqrstuvwxyz

Grid ten by ten

And words of three."

Suddenly in front of Ben appeared a grid of letters.

"Now," said Richard, "to get rid of it you have to find the words."

"But what if I can't?" asked Ben.

"Then it'll stay in front of you forever." Richard smiled, "and don't go asking me for help. It's just a jumbled up bunch of letters as far as I can see."

The old magician continued to walk through the forest laughing as he did so. Adder arrived beside Ben.

"How many words have you got to find?" he asked

Ben placed his finger on an S and ran it down to the right in a diagonal line over the letters S-W-A-L-L-O-W. The word SWALLOW glowed yellow.

"Only two to go."

The boy stared at the grid. He was good at these back home. Suddenly he spotted another one and pointed it out the same way as before. R-O-B-I-N.

"How do you know what you're looking for?" enquired the snake.

"They're all birds or plants."

Ben placed his finger on the R of ROBIN again then moved it down in a straight line. R-O-S-E.

The word glowed yellow before the entire grid faded away.

"Come on," said Adder, "we haven't got all day."

The boy straightened the bag on his shoulder and set about catching up with Richard.

What started, as a distant noise became a thunderous roar as the party of three emerged from the woodland into a clearing beside an enormous waterfall.

123

The River Sentence from its source high up in the Anagram Mountains flowed quickly, twisting and turning its way through the Paragraph Forest until it joined the Punctuation Sea. On its way it passed many villages and towns, but before it reached any of them the waters dropped over thirty metres down, crashing onto rocks and spraying anything that dared to come close. At this point the river was twenty metres wide with water flowing so fast it would be impossible to cross with a boat.

"Welcome!" shouted Richard extending his right arm to invite his guests to the view, "to Word Falls!"

Ben gazed at the site; it was much, much large than Marywitch Falls. The roaring noise generated from the powering waters flowing over the top and plummeting down to the rocks below made it difficult for the young lad to even hear himself.

On the other side of the falls, through the mist of the spray that even at this height was managing to get them damp, Ben could see a path.

"Is that where we need to get too?" he shouted.

"Yes!" came the reply from Richard.

Adder looked over at the old man whom, aside from his beard and long grey hair, was starting to look younger. "And how are we going to get over there?"

"Simple!" Began Mr Lexiur, "We Cross-Word Falls!"

Ben and Adder just looked at each other neither of them with a clue as to what the old man was talking about. Richard realised that they didn't understand and came to the conclusion that a demonstration would be preferable to an explanation.

He walked over to a rock sited by the side of the flowing water then turned and beckoned his comrades over. The boy and the snake complied and moved over to where Richard was starting.

"This rock," he said pointing at the stone, "was charmed many, many years ago. It activates a Cross-Word Spell."

He then placed his hand on the rock.

"I have to go

From this ridge.

And solve the clues

Of the Crossword Bridge."

A number of empty boxes appeared in front of the falling water creating a path over to the other side.

Richard stood there with a big smile on his face. "Now all we have to do is solve the clues, spell out the words and they will fill in the boxes for us to climb over."

"What clues?" asked Ben.

No sooner had he asked the question and in the mist hanging over the falls the first clue appeared written in what looked like clouds.

"One Down: Seven Letters" they spelt out, "To go forward?"

Adder looked confused, "Describe what?"

"ADVANCE!" called out Ben, "A-D-V-A-N-C-E"

The letters appeared in the first seven boxes leading down the drop from where they were standing.

"Advance means to move forward," Ben said waiting for the next clue to appear.

"I knew you were an English expert," said Adder.

Ben didn't acknowledge the snake's comment with a response. He just stood there waiting for the next clue. He could see from the position boxes that the next word would begin with a V.

The cloud words started to form again. Ben read the clue out loud.

"Two Across: Seven Letters: To Shake."

"Shudder!" yelled Adder.

"   It starts with a V," Ben said slightly annoyed, pointing at the point where the word was going to start.

"Vibrate?" said Richard, "But I wouldn't be able to spell it."

"How have you got across here in the past, Richard?" asked Adder.

"I've always had someone with me." Richard sounded slightly embarrassed.

"V-I-B-R-A-T-E!" shouted Ben.

The letters filled the gaps creating half the bridge.

"Don't worry about it Mr Lexiur," said Ben, "We wouldn't be here without you."

This made Richard feel important and he shook off any of the doubts he'd had about himself.

"Right," Ben said looking at Adder, "this one has five letters with T being the third one."

The cloud letters began to form again and, like before, Ben read them out.

"Three Down: Five Letters: Could be letters could be music."

"I think I know this one," said Adder smiling.

"Go on." Said Ben.

"Fives letters?" Adder continued.

"Yes."

"Third letter being T?"

Ben was becoming impatient, "Just say the word Adder!"

"Notes", he said with a big smile, "You have musical notes and you write a Note to someone, otherwise known as a letter."

"Very good, Adder," said Richard.

Ben patted his friend on the back then spelt out the word, "N-O-T-E-S."

The letters appeared creating a ladder. The last word would end with N. The cloud writing changed for the last time.

"Four Across: Nine Letters: Not Remembered."

A blank look fell across Adder's face. With this clue he was going to be no use whatsoever. Richard scratched his head.

"I know this," he said, "It's on the tip of my tongue."

He pulled a face, twisted his beard up in his hand, panted and groaned. He did everything he could to get the word out of his head. He even tried slapping himself on the forehead to see if that would dislodge it, but no.

"It's no use," he said dejected, "I've forgotten it."

"That's it!" shouted Ben excited, "you got it!"

"Got what?" asked Richard.

"Forgotten. F-O-R-G-O-T-T-E-N."

The last letters reached out to the bank on the other side. The party of three all cheered and hugged each other before advancing onto the crossing.

They climbed down Advance as far as the V then crossed over Vibrate before climbing up the first three letters of Notes. Adder smiled with a moment of pride when they reached this point.

Once at the top they strolled along Forgotten from N to F. Finally they were on the other side. As Adder, the last of the party, slithered off the last letter the Cross-Word Bridge melted away into the misty spray of the falls.

"Not far now," said Richard leading the way up the path, "the Gorge is just down here."

Adder and Ben gave each other a knowing glance, hopefully they had made up enough time to catch up with Anna and stop her once and for all. Ben followed Richard down the path with Adder, as always, bringing up the rear.

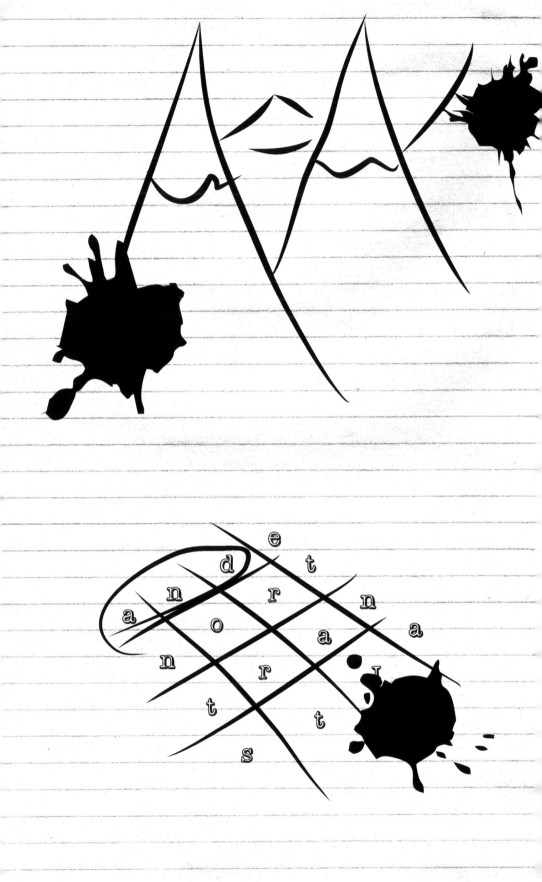

Chapter WX

The Palindrome Gorge was a gap in the Anagram Mountains with high rocky sides reaching up one hundred metres. It was named because it did not matter whether you were coming at it from the Snrevac Caverns or the Paragraph Forest, the entrances look identical. They looked so alike that you had to turn around to see what's behind you in order to tell which end you were at.

The path from the forest left the tree line some twenty metres from the vast V shape of the gorge and continued through to the caverns winding in an S. Nothing grew in the gorge. It was a barren desolate place.

The Snrevac Caverns at the other end were no better; a cold hash network of caves honeycombing the lower regions of Mount Grammar. Mount Grammar was the tallest of the peaks and had been the site of many a monstrous tale. The party knew if Anna reached the destination before them, she would disappear beneath the mountain with nothing else to think about but her spells and she would make it impossible for the jumbled up words to be corrected, or for the colour to be restored to language.

Ben stood admiring the power of the rock faces; it was truly awe-inspiring. Richard had started his way down the Gorge. Adder turned to Ben and told him to come along.

"We need to get to the mouth of the caverns," he said bringing Ben back to reality, "we should be able to cut her off there."

Ben followed Adder quickening his step so as to catch up with the Word Magician. Once in the gorge itself Ben felt quite claustrophobic. The high walls seemed to bear down on him and seemed to actually be moving in closer. He concentrated on the light brown dusty path decorated with the occasional pebble. It took his attention away from the imposing valley sides. The light around them was fading fast as night sky grew darker.

They were making good pace along the path when suddenly Richard stopped.

"Did you hear that?" he whispered.

They all listened attentively. Echoing on the wind blowing from the direction of Mount Grammar there was, what seemed to Ben, the sound of a laugh. It was not any old laugh. It was that cold hard cackle he had heard back at the palace. Queen Anna Gram had arrived first and was ahead of them.

Richard and Ben started to run while Adder slithered very quickly. The fact that she was laughing meant she thought she'd got away. Soon they were at the other end of the gorge; there stood in front of the gaping cavern entrance was Anna. Her silver dress glistened in the moonlight. Her green hair was silky and smooth.

She turned to look at her hunters. Ben could feel her deep blue eyes penetrate deep into his mind again. This time he knew what was happening and shook his head to free himself.

Adder moved forward, "It's time to end this Anna."

The Queen took a step towards the General, "Remember this place snake," she raised her arms and spun around as if she was showing the mountain to a prospective buyer. "It was here I got away before."

"Not this time!" Adder raised his tail and started to swirl it around. The tip began to glow a bright orange, "I will not make the same mistake twice."

Anna narrowed her eyes, "You just did!"

She thrust her right hand forward, forks of lightning shot out in every direction from her fingertips and a large gust of wind, similar to the one that slammed the door on them in the palace only stronger, blew straight at them. The gust was strong enough to make Adder lose his balance. The snake stumbled back tripped on a rock and fell over.

Ben's eyes squinted in empathy as Adder's head bounced of a large hard angled boulder. The glow of his tail burst into a bright flash before fading away to nothing, Adder's eyes closed.

"You should just cast your spell," said Anna in a gloating tone, "instead of talking, snake."

Tears welled up in Ben's eyes to a point that his lower lids could no longer contain the fluid. He could feel the water run down his face. The boy ran over to his friend and held him in his arms; he was still breathing. Anger filled every ounce of his being; this was more than he could bear.

"What's the matter, little boy?" Anna's voice tore into Ben like broken glass, "is your ikkle snake friend hurt?"

Ben stood up; he had counted to ten several times in his head already and was just starting another run through. He knew that if she ran in to those caverns she would be lost to him forever and retribution and justice would not be served.

He had an idea but wasn't sure if it would work. Once he had counted his final ten he raised his right arm.

"The number of caves in the Snrenvac Caverns divide by one hundred, round down and show me the answer."

From behind Anna the sound of rocks cracking and scraping echoed forth. She turned to see what was happening. Once the sound had ceased Ben repeated the spell. Again cracking and scraping noises emanated from within the mountain caves.

"No!" screamed Anna seeing the outcome of the spell.

The moon was bright and illuminated the cavern entrance. Ben said the spell again. Richard smiled seeing the effects of Ben's work, each time the boy cast the Divide spell the number of caves reduced.

Ben didn't know how many caves there were in there, he figured that if he cast it enough eventually there would be only one left. Anna had the same thought; she turned and threw a gust of wind at the boy.

The air movement caused him to stumble, he turned so that his back was to the wind and managed to regain his balance.

"Ben, quick!" shouted Richard.

Ben turned back to face the evil Queen only she had gone. Whilst his back was turned she had run into the caves. Ben ran forward to enter but before he could get there a howl so loud and so full of despair came out of the darkness of the caverns.

He took his torch out of his bag and shone it into the darkness. His plan had worked, the honeycomb system of caverns had been reduced to one big cave. The entrance where he stood was the only way in or out. Sat in the very centre, with her silver dress spread out around her, Anna wept – but not with sorrow.

She raised her head to confront her tormentor. Ben had seen that look of anger many times in the eyes of his teachers or parents when he had done something stupid, though he had never seen anger so intense. Ben backed up so that he no longer stood in the cave itself.

Anna bent the fingers on both her hands as if she was pulling fists but only making them half way. Then she brought her hands up to face each other with a gap between them. Sparks crackled from the ends of her fingers, jumping the void from fingertip to fingertip. A small ball of flame appeared in the space between her palms. As she pulled her hands apart the flame grew until it was the size of a football.

The evil queen looked at Ben, the orange glow of the fireball tinted her pale skin; she smiled.

"Never send a boy," her voice was full of hate, "to do a snake's job!"

Ben was frozen to the spot, he wanted to move but his legs felt like they had been turned to stone. Anna raised her elbows so that they were level with the flame then, throwing her arms forward and flicking her wrists, she hurled the fireball across the cave towards the entrance, towards Ben.

A moment of stillness, that would have lasted less than a second but felt to Ben like a minute, passed as the boy watched the fiery missile leave the launch pad of Anna's hands. Suddenly something hit him hard in the back. He fell forward, face in the dirt.

The ball of flame flew over his head. He could feel the heat emanating from it as it passed over. Having just pushed Ben to the floor, Richard was now in path of the fireball which hit him in the chest.

The collision threw the old man a full three metres back towards the gorge. Ben looked round from his prone position. Light wisps of smoke snaked their way towards the sky from Richard's singed facial hair. Ben pulled himself up onto his hands and knees. Anna cackled before copying the motions that brought about the creation of the first fireball.

"I don't miss twice, boy!"

Ben quickly got to his feet, he wanted to retort to her jibe, however, he remembered the advice she had give to Adder. 'You should just cast your spell instead of talking.' He knew what he had to do: take her attention away from everything else. Richard had told him that she was obsessed with scrambling all words.

He raised his right hand towards Anna,

"For Anna Gram A word search be,

With every word in the dictionary,

Reading horizontal, vertical and diagonally,

The number of words same as the grid equally,

The size of the grid..."

Ben paused, he had a number in his head but the idea seemed so cruel. This was the only way to stop her as far as he could see and with both Adder and Richard injured there was no one around he could take advice from.

Anna laughed, "There's your mistake boy!"

She threw the fireball, which headed towards Ben a great speed. This time he was ready, he twisted to his right and learned back. The heat from the flames, as they passed across the front of his chest, made Ben close his eyes. Now he was certain. He straightened up knowing that this was the right thing to do.

"What are you going to do?" Anna smiled, "I can solve any Word Search you throw at me. I'll find every word and jumbled them up.

"That's what I'm counting on," Ben's eyes narrowed.

"The size of the grid, Infinity by Infinity!"

As soon as the last word was uttered the cave began to fill with letters. They immediately took Anna's attention; Ben could see the look on her face, nothing else mattered to her, she had to find the words.

Within seconds she had found and scrambled Aardvark, house and November. However, no sooner had she discovered these words than another thousand letters containing another hundred words appeared. The look of determination she had worn in the beginning now turned to one of sheer panic.

More and more letters formed in the grid. Frantically she tried to find to words but it was too much. Her obsession meant she couldn't stop and with the task growing bigger and bigger by the second, she started to scream.

"NO!" Her wail reverberated around the cave and out of the entrance, "I MUST FIND THEM ALL!"

Suddenly a voice came from behind Ben, "A self perpetuating Word Search grid." It was Richard. "I like it."

"Richard! You're alive!" Ben ran over to the old man who was now sitting upright, though his beard had been shortened considerably by the fireball.

The young lad helped the old man to his feet. Richard coughed then ensured Ben he was all right.

"We have to seal the cave," he said.

"I don't know how to," replied Ben.

"I can help with that," Adder's voice groggily announced.

Ben smiled wider than he had ever smiled before. He ran over to his friend and gave him a big hug. Adder wrapped his tail round the boy and returned the gesture.

The snake rubbed his head then made his way to the front of the cave. Inside the scrambler of words was possessed by the futile task in front of her.

Adder raised his tail, the end began to glow orange. He pointed at the rock face above the entrance to the cave.

"Stand back," he told the other two.

Ben and Richard backed up to a safe distance. A bolt of orange lightning shot forth from Adder, hitting the rock face. The noise of crumbling stone filled the air and Adder move sharply back to join the others.

The front of the cave began to fill with falling rocks. As the pile grew bigger and bigger, Anna's cries grew quieter and quieter. Before long the entire entrance was covered leaving no gaps, and the desperate sounds of the evil queen had gone.

The silence of the night hung over the party of three for a moment before being broken by the distant sound of the night animals coming from the forest at the other end of the gorge. It was the first time Ben had heard any wildlife since arriving in these parts.

"I think the spell's have been broken," he said.

Adder smiled, "Yet again Ben you have saved the day."

Ben looked over at Richard, "Thank you," he said.

"What for?" asked Richard.

"You saved my life and gave me the knowledge to defeat Anna Gram."

The old man looked embarrassed by Ben's gratitude, "It was nothing."

"I think," said Adder, "we should move to the other end of the gorge and set up camp on the edge of the forest for the night."

The others agreed that this was a good idea. Richard took the lead with Adder this time walking beside him. Ben straightened his bag on his shoulder and looked at the sealed entrance of the cave. He felt guilty about what he had done but knew it was the only way to stop her. He looked up at the stars then, by the command of Adder calling back and telling him to hurry up, ran down the path to join them.

The cold air had gone and the night was pleasant. The three of them found a nice flat spot by the tree line and lay down. Ben's head was full of thoughts and question but the excitement of the day was too much and before he realised it, he was asleep.

Chapter YZ

The sun rose above Diction Land and with Anna Gram's influence removed, its warmth beat down upon the land putting an end to the unnatural cold that had gripped these parts. The flowers, tree and bushes felt the difference, as did the forest wildlife.

The birds, having found places to hide, came out and flew into the treetops. They were happy that warmth had returned and, at the very tops of their voices, sang out to tell the rest of the lands.

Ben opened his eyes; the sound of the birdsong had awakened him. He stretched out his arms and legs and yawned loudly.

"Morning," greeted Richard.

He had been so early out of his slumber that he could have easily beaten any of the birds to the worms had he wished to do so. Adder was also awake, the sun's warm rays had made him aware of the morning; he also greeted Ben after the boy's noises had indicated his entry to the day.

They all sat for a while taking in their surroundings; with the warm air the forest looked beautiful. Ben was astounded how different things could look when it wasn't cold anymore.

Richard stood up and looked down the path which led back to the Word Falls.

"I think it's time for me to go home."

"But Richard," said Ben, "you have to help us correct all the words."

Richard smiled, "Walk with me to my house, we'll have some tea and talk about it."

Adder slithered over to Richard and beckoned Ben to join them. The young lad obliged and soon the three of them were walking through the woodland.

Instead of heading back over the falls Richard led them down a path less travelled. There was definitely a track there but it was terribly overgrown.

They walked in silence through the undergrowth deeper and deeper into the forest. The birds were still singing and signs of life that previously had been absent were all around them.

Ben was curious about Adder. In his confrontation with Anna both the snake and the queen had referred to the last time. According to the book Ben had read back in Alphabet City the last she had been in these parts was many, many years ago. So how old is he? Ben thought.

He quickened his step to walk beside his friend.

"Adder?" he started.

"Yes, Ben," the snake replied with his usual lisp.

"How old are you?"

"It is not polite to ask a snake his age," Adder said, wearing a coy smile.

"It's just that back when you were talking to Anna you…" Ben did not have the chance to finish his line of questioning.

"I have been around for some time," Adder said, "and thanks to you I will be around for some time more."

Ben went to ask another question but before he could utter a word Adder stopped him.

"There are many lands in this world as there are many in your own." Adder stopped and placed his tail on Ben's shoulder, "And I'm sure you're going to see a lot of them, here and at home."

Ben looked deep into Adder's eyes. There was more to this snake than he had ever contemplated, and there was certainly more than his scaly friend was letting on. Adder winked at Ben then without another word continued to follow the old magician. Ben just shook his head.

"I will find out one day," he whispered to himself before also continuing the journey.

It felt to Ben as if they had been walking for more than an hour when they reached a clearing in the forest. Sited in the centre of a large round well-kept field was a small white walled cottage with a black slate roof. The window frames for both the upstairs and ground floor were also painted black as was the frame around the bright red front door. The garden surrounding the cottage was full of flowers blooming in a variety of colours.

Richard led them down the path, through the little yellow gate in the white picket fence and welcomed them to his home. He opened the front door and beckoned his guests inside.

The hallway was tight due to the floor-to-ceiling bookshelf that ran down the right hand side. Ben looked at a few of the titles but none of them made any sense to him at all; it was like a foreign language. Richard could see Ben struggling and explained.

"When I read normal words they look all jumbled up to me."

"I know," said Ben. "And jumbled up words read correctly to you."

Just then Ben understood why he couldn't read any of the book titles.

"So you jumbled up the words in these books?" Ben said pointing at the tomes.

"Yes," answered Richard, "so I can read them."

The old man beckoned his guests to turn left before reaching the stairs that led up to the next floor. Adder was first to enter the living room followed very closely by Ben.

More books took up most of the space in there; again all the words in them had been jumbled so Richard could enjoy their contents. Two red leather high backed Windsor chairs sat opposite each other slightly turned towards the deep redwood fireplace. In the corner of the room was a wooden rocking chair facing the window that overlooked the garden. Sunlight was bursting into the room from the window and Ben watched as the dust, now unsettled, danced in its beams. Richard called into the room as he passed the door on his way to the kitchen.

"I'll just put some tea on."

Adder turned the rocking chair to face the room before making himself comfortable in it; Ben sat down in one of the leather chairs. After some clunking and bagging, followed by a kettle whistle, Richard entered carrying a tray.

He placed the tray down on the floor between the chairs and poured three cups of tea. Adder came over to add his own milk and sugar; Ben, being closer, just leant forward to do the same.

The three of them sat chatting about what had transpired the night before, enjoying their cuppa as well as each other's company. Ben finished his drink and placed the cup back on the tray.

"So how do we unscramble all the words?" asked the boy.

Richard sat back in his seat and took in a deep breath,

"You have to visit each village and cast the Solve Anagram spell." He stared Ben straight in the eye, "As each village is corrected the colour will return, by the time you get back to Alphabet City, all colour will have returned to language and the city will be back to normal."

He reached over to a pile of books on his right. After a few seconds sifting through the titles the wise old Word Magician removed a book.

"Watch," he said, bringing the book to his lap.

"This book title reveal the sham,

It's time to solve the anagram."

He waved his hand over the book cover as he spoke. Ben watched as the book title rearranged itself so instead of reading A Nag Mall Press it read Anagram Spells.

Richard smiled, "Just use this spell at each village naming the type of words that live there."

Ben nodded showing his teacher he understood. Adder stood up and walked across the room to stand beside Ben.

"We really should be going," he said. "We have a lot of work to do."

Richard agreed and made his way to the front door to wish his friends a good journey. Ben and adder stood on the doorstep saying their goodbyes. Richard extended his right hand and offered it to Ben.

"I know you can do it, lad," he said shaking Ben's hand. "It has been a real joy to meet you.

"Likewise," said Ben.

"And Adder," he let go of Ben's hand and took the snake's tail to afford him the same gesture. "As always, it's been a pleasure."

Adder smiled, "Let's hope the next time we meet it will be under better circumstances."

"You always say that," retorted Richard smiling.

Adder laughed, shook Richard's hand once more, then beckoned Ben to follow him. Before they could get to the yellow gate Richard called them back. They stopped and turned to see the old man making his way up the garden path.

"Ben," he said offering the boy something he was holding, "I think you should have this."

He handed Ben a small silver upper-case A pin badge. Ben smiled and thanked his new friend before attaching the letter to the lapel of his blazer, just under his gold infinity symbol. He thanked the magician again before following Adder across the field to another overgrown path. At the tree line they turned back for one last wave goodbye. Richard reciprocated the farewell with exaggerated arm movements.

Adder suggested that the first village they visit should be Noun being as they were the first to be affected by Anna's spell and had been messed up the longest. Ben agreed; he was looking forward to meeting the Proper Nouns again and finding out what their name actually are.

"So Adder," Ben began, curious about something Richard had said when they were leaving. "How long have you known Mr Lexiur?"

"Oh we go back a long way," said Adder not giving anything away.

The two carried on walking in the direction Adder suggested, chatting away about this and that. Ben would occasionally fish for information about Adder's past but the clever old snake was too smart and his coy answers left Ben with even more questions.

They crossed over Sentence River at a little wooden footbridge much further down river from the Word Falls. The path continued twisting through the undergrowth, Ben was quite lost though he had complete faith that Adder knew where he was going so didn't worry.

The conversations helped pass the time and before they knew it the sun was in position for early evening. This coincided with Ben and Adder reaching the edge of Noun.

The damage caused when the Raid Pestgin attacked was evident. The giant spider had felled trees in its wake. Large areas now resembled a giant sized version of the game Pick up sticks, with tree trunks replacing the thin straws.

They entered the village, walking down the main street; the place was deserted. Ben took the lead and walked up to the small shop on the corner where he first entered the village a couple of days ago. The sign reading Ice Off Stop swung lightly in the breeze from the grey building. Ben turned to the look at the village, raised his right hand and cast the spell.

"These Nouns, reveal the sham,

It's time to solve the anagram."

No sooner had he finished saying the last word than the sign on the wall changed, its letters moved around to reveal the shop's true name: Post

Office. The building it hung from started to change too. The dark grey of the door faded to a bright red, the light grey stone of the shop washed over with a yellow. Even the sign filled with colour, no longer dark grey letters on a light grey background, now it was red letters on a yellow background.

In fact the whole village was changing colour. Bright blues and greens, Purples and Pinks every colour in the rainbow was there. The door of the Post Office opened and out came a bright red word with a bag over its shoulder. Ben recognised the bag but instead of the word reading Tampson as it had on his first visit the word now read Postman.

"I know who I am!" said the Postman, excited. "The spell has been lifted!"

More and more words came out of their brightly coloured houses. Soon the streets were full of naming words full of colour and life.

"We must go and see the Pro Nouns," Ben said to Adder.

The two of them pushed their way through the celebrating words toward the round building in the centre of the village. Stood outside with big grins on their faces were the Proper Nouns. Noty was now a deep blue Tony, Cluy had become a beautiful bright pink Lucy and Linco a proud purple Colin. Once they saw Ben they got very excited and ran over to him.

"Ben my boy," said Tony. "You're alive!"

"We thought you were dead for sure," said Lucy giving him a kiss on the check.

Colin just grabbed hold of the lad and gave him the biggest hug he'd ever had. Ben was a bit embarrassed by all the attention but fully understood why they were all so happy.

"Come," said Lucy, "you must join us to help us celebrate the lifting of the spell."

"I sorry," said Ben, "but we have to remove the spell from all the other villages as soon as possibly."

"It's getting late," said Adder. "We might as well stay here the night and go to the other villages at first light."

"That's a great idea," enthused Colin.

Ben and Adder joined in the party for a while before leaving the Nouns to get on with it. They had another long day ahead of them and sleep was very important. They requested a bed near the outskirts of the village so they could be as far away from the noisy celebrations as possible. Colin organised this with no problem, the owner of the small house, a green word called owner, was intending to party all night long and declared he didn't 'need his bed' before laughing out loud and running off to dance with a rather pretty looking lavender Girl.

The party raged on through the night. Ben and Adder were too tired to be bothered by noise anyway and soon fell fast asleep.

At first light the two were up and ready to go. They walked through the centre of Noun, words were lying asleep on the street, and it looked like the party had only just finished. Some nouns were still up. Owner was now dancing on his own and a couple of Bushes, the words not the plants, were finishing off the last of the buffet.

They didn't stop to speak to anyone, time was very much of the essence and so quietly, without any fuss, they left.

It took them at least two hours to reach Verb. The village was in much the same disarray as Noun had been, the builds had no colour, nor did the jumbled up occupants. Ben cast the spell only this time replacing the word noun with the word verb.

The spell worked again with the same effect as before. The building became bright colours and the residents began doing what Verbs do best: doing things. They celebrated their freedom from the spell by working, digging and building.

Ben and Adder didn't waste any time; they set about the path leading to

Adjective. It was well past lunchtime when they got to their destination. To describe the town would be folly as it was no different from the others. The same spell was cast, with the same variation to include adjective, with the same outcome. The words here were not just bright in colour but also in the words they described. Every colour, texture and size lived here.

Ben was happy with their achievements and so the two moved on. They repeated the same saving spell in Adverb, another hour down the road from Adjective, freeing all words that describe what, when, where, how and time.

It was moving from day to night by the time Ben and Adder had finished removing the spell from all the villages. They decided, being as it would take them at least four hours to get back to the city, that camping out under the stars would be the best option. They found a spot in a small clearing, made themselves comfortable and, after saying goodnight to each other, rested their heads after another very long but rewarding day.

The journey back to the city was very warm. Now the cold was gone the sun had nothing stopping it. Not long after they had started walking Ben removed his blazer and hung it over his arm. Adder had a very good knowledge of the region and finding the city was no problem.

The great walls surrounding Alphabet City were very different to the ones Ben had left behind. Instead of looking like cold grey stone they were in fact sand coloured. The boy and the snake approached the small door which lead to the courtyard round the back of the building Ben had departed from many days ago.

Adder twisted the handle, pushed open the door and entered. Ben sheepishly followed; he was worried there might be loads of people here waiting to thank them. Even though it was the last thing he wanted, a small twinge of disappointment brushed over him when he found the courtyard to be empty.

The back of the building looked splendid, various blues, yellows and reds creating a terrific sight. Adder crossed over the courtyard to the entrance of the building. Just as he was about reach out for the handle, Z came bursting through the door. He was well and truly back to his old deep ruby red self. From behind the leader of letters two very familiar face appeared: Pi, the maths symbol looked at Ben before suddenly being pushed to one side by Exclamation Mark making his way past and running over to the boy.

"BEN!" shouted Exclaim, "IT'S SO GOOD TO SEE YOU!"

Ben smiled and greeted his joyous companions with an expression of happiness that couldn't be missed. Adder then called over to Pi. Having been pushed to one side the old symbol hadn't seen his friend standing by the door. Pi embraced the snake with many comments on how it was good to see him. Adder returned the sentiments.

"I'm sorry to be a party pooper but…" Ben had a solemn tone, "I really should be getting home. I've been gone for almost a week."

"But we've been planning a celebration," said Z.

Pi then spoke, "They've had the N horse specially groomed to take you and Adder on a victory tour."

"We've been organising it since the weather got warmer," Z continued, "and then after we had word from Noun we knew you'd be back very soon."

"WE HAVE JELLY AND ICE CREAM AS WELL!" shouted Exclaim.

Ben was caught in two minds. On one hand he really wanted to go home, it had been a long time since he'd seen his friends and his parents, but on the other the letters had gone to so much trouble he felt bad if he didn't accept their hospitality. Adder slithered over to him and whispered in his ear.

"Don't worry about the time," he said, "I'll sort it."

"Can we just do the victory parade?" asked Ben.

"Whatever you want to do," replied Adder with a soothing tone.

Ben told Z and the others that he would ride in the victory parade but wouldn't stay for the night's celebration. Z looked disappointed but understood.

"Well then," he said, "will you accept use of the horse and cart to get you home quicker?"

Ben smiled and thanked Z for the kind gesture.

"That would be great!"

The party then entered the building, which was now full of colour, and followed Z through the corridors turning left and right until they reached the front. As they exited the main doors a massive roar exploded from the waiting crowd.

Every available space on the street was taken by letters and punctuation marks wanting to get a glimpse of the heroes. Ben and Adder waved to the crowd though Ben felt very uncomfortable with all the attention.

The council of Vowels, who had been so mean to Ben when he first arrived, were now full of colour and good cheer. Ben, Adder, Pi and Z climbed aboard the N horse drawn coach that was parked outside the main entrance. The N horses were a lovely deep brown and the lowercase d driver was no longer pastel but a proud royal blue. He tipped his cap at Ben.

"Good to see you again sir"

With a flick of his wrists the d signalled the N horses to advance down the road.

"Walk on!"

The city was beautiful, the colours in the building and the people were bright and happy. Every corner they turned, every street they drove down, people were cheering and waving flags. Z told the driver that the parade was going to end at the main gate instead of the main square.

"But what about the jelly and ice cream?" asked d.

"Oh," answered Ben, "you can still have that."

The driver smiled then returned his attention to the road. As the carriage pulled round the final corner Ben could see the building he thought looked like a church but instead of being all dark and grey, it was gold, glistening in the bright sunshine.

"Woah there!"

The driver pulled up alongside the guardhouse. Z told the driver that Adder would take over the reins as they were borrowing the carriage to get them home quicker. The driver did as he was asked, dipping his cap again as he bade the travellers farewell. Adder climbed up front to take control of the N horses.

"Are you sure I can't tempt you to stay for a little while longer?" Z asked Ben as he prepared to exit the carriage.

"I'm quite sure," insisted Ben, "but thank you for the offer."

Z climbed down and ordered the gates to be opened. A number of guards ran about the place shouting at each other before two large doors opened in the side of the guard house. As they did Ben could see the main gates had also been opened showing the path leading back up into the hills.

"Walk on!" commanded Adder flicking the reins in the same manner as the driver had.

The N horses walked forward through the doors and then through the gates. The sounds of the Alphabet City's citizens could still be heard for some time after they'd left. Soon they had travelled far enough for the noise to disappear off into the distance.

Pi enquired as to what happened. Ben sat back in his seat and told Pi a tale of giant spiders, evil queens and a great Word Magician. Pi proclaimed he'd never hear the like. Ben continued his story with great enthusiasm. He was so involved in its telling that he hadn't noticed how far they'd travelled. By the time Ben realised where they were Adder had already crossed the boundary

abcdefghijklmnopqrstuvwxyz

at the top of the hill and was making good progress down the green Zero Path towards Mathamagical.

"Blimey," said Ben, "are we here already?"

"Woah There!"

Adder pulled the carriage to a halt. He turned to look at his passengers.

"This is the spot," he said to Ben.

Ben could see the signpost pointing towards the city of Mathamagical, he knew exactly where he was. He said his goodbye to Pi and promised he'd be back again soon.

"Though next time it will be just a social visit," he said.

"I'm sure it will," responded Pi, "surely you can't have a dangerous adventure every time you come here?"

Ben laughed at the notion then climbed down from the back of the carriage. Adder had already drawn the infinity sign the air with his tail, Ben could see his classroom through the opening it created.

"I've used a little time magic," said Adder.

"Time Magic?" questioned Ben.

"Just a little something I picked up from another land," Adder said with a grin, "It has allowed me to open the door just after the time you left, so back home you won't have been gone very long at all."

"So it's still morning break?!"

"If that was the time you left, yes."

Ben smiled and gave Adder a big hug.

"I'll see you soon," said Adder.

With a nod of agreement Ben stepped forward back into the science room.

"If it's still morning break I can get to my next lesson?"

He started to run towards the classroom door but it was much further away than he remembered. *You idiot*, he thought, *I haven't reversed the ratio spell!*

"Ten to one, one to ten," he started, "Grow Ben Small to this ratio."

The sickly feeling he had before returned to his stomach. Everything around him reduced in size, as he grew bigger. Soon he was back to his normal self. He rummaged through his bag to find his timetable, highlighted in green it showed him his next lesson.

"Half an hour of English"

No time to waste he ran out of the science room and down the corridor as quickly as he could. He grabbed the handle of the double doors leading to the stairs that would take him down and pulled.

As he opened the door the body of a man came tumbling through scattering papers all over the place. It was Mr Trot, again! He was just about to push the door open with his back, being as his arms were full of the papers he was carrying, when Ben had pulled it open. With the door not there anymore the science teacher had nothing to stop him and, as before, was now surrounded by paper on the floor.

Mr Trot looked up at Ben, he looked very angry indeed, "You again Small!"

"I'm sorry sir."

The teacher picked himself up, and started to gather up his papers.

"Well don't just stand there!"

Ben knelt down next to the teacher and helped him gather his stuff together. Mr Trot couldn't tell Ben off for opening the door, there was no way he could have known what was on the other side. He thanked Ben for his help and warned him about running in the corridors.

"I know sir," said Ben, "I won't sir."

"Right then," said Mr Trot composing himself, "You'd better head towards your next class, the bell will be going any second. Oh and did you get what you wanted for the head master?"

"What sir?" for a second Ben had forgotten the story he gave to the teacher on their previous encounter. "Oh no sir, it wasn't there."

"Oh well!"

Mr Trot continued his way back to his classroom, just then the bell rang for the end of morning break. Ben walked quickly to his next lesson. Everything seemed very surreal, here he had only been gone ten minutes yet to him it felt like he'd been away for a week.

He entered Mrs Dockly's class a little after everyone else had already taken their seats. She didn't look pleased at his late arrival even though he was less than a minute late.

"Glad you could join us Mr Small," she said in a very sarcastic way.

"Where have you been?" asked Danny.

"I'll tell you later." whispered Ben.

Mrs Dockly gave the boy a very stern stare.

"Right!" she said to the entire class, "Can anybody tell me what this word is?"

With her chalk she wrote on the blackboard MANARAG. Ben started to laugh. The teacher turned round looking very annoyed.

"Do you find it funny?"

"No miss." Ben tried to hold back his amusement.

"Well then, maybe you can tell me what it says?" she tapped the stick of chalk on the blackboard under the word.

"It's an anagram miss," said Ben, "of the word anagram."

abcdefghijklmnopqrstuvwx**yz**

She looked at the board then back at Ben, in all her years of teaching she never had a pupil get the answer right first time. Ben smiled trying his best to look as surprised as she was.

"Yes," she said, "it is an anagram of the word anagram…"

She continued to waffle on about how anagram's work and what they're all about. Ben sat back in his chair and rubbed the silver upper-case A pinned to his lapel and smiled; this was going to an easy lesson, he thought.

Ben and Adder will return in
TICK-TOCK-A-HOLICK

21381312R00094

Printed in Great Britain
by Amazon